Where Wolves TALK

By D. L. Lewis

Illustrated by D. L. Lewis

Dedicated to my mother and father, Tashina the Wolf, Sunbeam the Arab/Quarter-Horse Cross, Kitten, and my faithful companion for 15 years: my Arab mare Carrin.

Table of Contents

Illustrations

CHAPTER ONE

The Conversation

"It's too much," sighed Kitten. "It's all just too much. Or maybe it isn't enough?" He sniffed in irritation and wiggled his hips, scrunching them down against the firm cushion of the chair he had chosen for his spell of *après*-breakfast repose. "Too much, yet not enough."

The little silver tiger tabby had everything, it seemed. The fortunate fellow had been blessed with a fabulous home in the country northeast of London; this grand mansion provided by his Lady, with over a hundred fascinating rooms to explore, and countless flights of stairs for dashing up and racing down. Along with the palatial digs came the exquisite sustenance the cooking staff lavished on the feline with loving care. Surely very few cats were lucky enough to dine on food fit for royalty; delicacies such as sweet fresh salmon flown in via helicopter from a remote Scottish loch and poached into pink perfection by the household's Swiss chef. This entrée was customarily followed by an antique plate of Sèvres porcelain bearing hunks of blue-veined Stilton. As Kitten licked the creamy cheese from his French dish's illustrated surface, he could enjoy a painted scene depicting Hercules in the act of capturing Cerberus; the vicious three-headed canine of Greek myth. Snatched from his guard post at the entrance to the underworld, the hideous dog snarled and struggled in enameled vain under the sandpaper friction of the tabby's rosy tongue.

Such an existence was the most pleasant and thoroughly civilized one a house cat could hope for; that much was certain. This particular house cat, however, spent a great deal of time at the mansion's windows; his glowing amber eyes staring with relentless longing at the wildlife that moved about through his Lady's forested garden. Yes; the wildlife: the Wild Life.

"It's too soft in this house!" Kitten muttered; the crisp white whiskers of his black-striped face trembling with frustration. "Too soft; too easy. There are no challenges for me anymore. True, there seemed to be things to achieve when I was just a wee babe: those courageous first flights up from the floor onto the tops of tables whose landscapes were utterly unknown to me. Yes, it was a thrill to soar onto mysterious plateaus which might hold great wonders or terrific dangers. But what did I find in those high places when I made the leaps? Silly things: heavy brass clocks who ticked mockingly at me yet failed to react even a jot when I slapped them soundly; electronic devices that whined and beeped in aimless confusion when I pushed them down onto the floor; vases which fell and shattered into a thousand dead shards with one solid swipe of my paw after putting up absolutely no fight whatsoever. Nonsensical, disappointing, too-easy things which offer no satisfaction at all to a noble feline: that is what I find when I spring up into the high places."

Kitten dug the claws of one forepaw into the brocade upholstery of the chair. Pulling his sharp talons out again, the annoyed predator studied the maroon and cream threads that clung to the hooked ends of his dangerous toenails, and tossed his head in disgust. "Look at that—the stringed guts of a helpless textile foe: the trophies of a coddled failure!" *Felis catus* snarled. "I was bred to be a great hunter, not a house-bound prisoner!"

Abandoning his position of rest, he jumped down onto one of the densely woven Oriental carpets that cushioned the cold marble floor of his Lady's huge library and strode across the grand room with the proud walk that showed the fortitude and strength of character with which the feline had conquered his several deformities. Bred in the States to be a top-notch show cat of the American Shorthair Silver Classic Tabby breed, something had gone awry in his genetic makeup; causing this otherwise beautiful little grey tiger to be born with a crooked spine that caused his ribs to jut out on one side, a rigidly curled tail set on his rear end like a furry wrong-way comma, and a distorted front left paw missing one of its main bones. Two of the pads on that foot were set at odd angles; one with its protruding talon poking out to the side, the other twisted under the foot so that the enlarged and flattened claw of that pad, clicking noisily against hard flooring, had given the tiny creature a sometimes audible walk that robbed him of a portion of the stealthy way of going in which ordinary cats revel. People felt sorry for Kitten when they saw these physical irregularities of his, but this outstanding member of the *Felidæ* family would have none of anyone's pity; strutting through life with the sturdy courage, graceful agility, and well-deserved pride of a Bengali jungle *tigris*.

As the feline marched across the room, heading for the exit to the corridor, the housekeeper entered the chamber; feather duster in one hand and soft cotton cloth in the other. As she drew near Kitten, he eyed the plump pink legs that showed below the hem of her black skirt.

"Now, there's a challenge!" he growled to himself. "She's far bigger than I, and can surely put up a better fight than a piece of dead furniture." He crouched down to gather impetus for the attacking spring, then leapt forward in a flying attack and threw himself onto the servant's left leg; clutching the solid appendage with all four cat-limbs. Clinging to his prey with the single-minded ferocity of a starving cheetah, *Felis catus* dug his merciless steel-trap jaws, armed with a very fine set of sharp white teeth, into the fleshy skin over the woman's shin bone.

A wild shriek of pain split the air, and the big grey feather duster came down to swoop at Kitten's head. Ducking in avoidance, the cat released his tooth-and-claw vise grip and circled around behind the woman to continue his assault from a more favorable angle. As he raised up to stand behind his opponent, the cat's fangs were bared in joyous menace; his claws were out and poised for gleeful slashing—he was at the ready; a tiny David primed for battle with this female Goliath.

"Kitten—no!" It was his Lady, standing in the doorway. The green-eyed brunette, a woman considered beautiful by many, wore a purple satin robe and carried a crystal perfume atomizer filled with water. She held the bottle up before her like a loaded pistol so the tabby could see it clearly. "No!" she repeated.

Recognizing the horrible device the Lady used as a threat to subdue strong-willed Kitten, the feline blinked and sat down on his haunches. He looked longingly at the housekeeper's tempting legs, then took a quick, furtive glance at the water sprayer, and blinked again. Water itself wasn't so very bad; in fact, Kitten liked to play with the light-reflecting substance as it dribbled from faucets or swirled noisily into the drains of bathtubs, but that hissing spray from the crystal atomizer: there was something about it which was quite simply intolerable.

After taking one more nervous, blinking look at the nasty bottle, Kitten scurried under a nearby couch, and the Lady disappeared from the doorway. Hidden within the low cave of sofa springs, fabric, and wood, the cat huddled in safety as the housekeeper bustled about the library making her employer's collection of antique books and other treasures spotlessly clean.

Crouched in his retreat, the tabby watched every move of the woman's big black-shod feet. "It would be so grand to run out there and start another battle," he thought, "but my Lady might be hiding in the corridor with that blasted spray monster." He shuddered; thinking of the horrors of the thing who hissed in that soft monotone "poooshh" and could spit a cloud of moisture onto his face in such disgustingly dreadful abundance. "I suppose everyone is afraid of something," he sighed. "I should not be ashamed of my fear of that one particularly awful thing."

Finished with her labors, the housekeeper exited the room. Kitten crawled out of his sanctuary and trotted to a stool set before a window offering a view of a bird feeder: a large wooden tray hung from an ancient yew near the house. It was early morning, and in the sunlight of the bright day, a large collection of fowl were busy at breakfast: some perched on the seed-filled feeder; others hopping about on the ground below it, pecking at tidbits which had fallen from above.

Springing up onto the stool, Kitten crouched down low and peered through the aged glass of the window. "Birds!" he declared. "Now, truly—those would be adversaries worthy of me. Perhaps they aren't as large or as strong as I, but they can fly, while I cannot. I would have to exercise a great deal of patience, intelligence, agility, and speed to capture one of those winged creatures."

He watched with the rapt attention of the born predator as a group of small blue-and-yellow birds hopped about on the grassy earth picking at insects.

6

The cat's curled tail twitched at its very end; the only flexible part of the genetically unusual appendage. About to burst from barely controlled excitement, the tabby emitted a crackling-ratcheting throat noise; the odd "ra-ahh-tat-tat-tat" sometimes spoken by felines who have spotted fascinating and unreachable prey.

This sound, soft as it was, did not escape the sensitive ears of one of the more watchful birds in the garden. A turtle dove seated on the feeder heard Kitten's cry of excitement and turned her head to better see the small tiger crouching behind the glass of the library window. "Cat!" she called to him.

Kitten started backwards in surprise; nearly falling off the stool. Recovering his balance quickly, he repeated his exclamation: "Ra-ahh-tat-tat-tat!"

The dove left the feeder and set herself down on the manicured grass below the window. "Stop that nonsense at once!" she commanded.

The tabby was rendered speechless by confusion. No bird had responded to his cries before. They either ignored him completely or flew away without a word—that was the norm; that was how things were supposed to be. An attempt at interchange—that was utterly out of the question: a radical alteration in the status quo of cat versus bird.

What was Kitten to do? Should a noble predator speak to the object of his hunting instinct? Of course not! That would be both unorthodox and undignified. What if someone important were to find out that he had spoken to a traditional adversary; engaging it in conversation? Horrified by the prospect of such blatant impropriety, he studied the elegant lines of the bird who stood on the ground below; looking up at him with an intelligent gaze.

The dove hopped up onto the window sill; her head now on a level with Kitten's. Fascinated, the cat moved forward as far as he could. Dove and Kitten were now eye to eye; separated by the pane of glass set in the window.

Kitten looked carefully at the bird. "That little head would fit into my mouth and possibly go down my throat quite nicely," he thought, "if only it weren't for that wretched glass between us."

"And why would you want to do that?" Dove inquired.

Kitten's surprise made him forget the rules of cat society, and he spoke aloud. "Why would I want to do what?"

"Eat my head, you silly creature."

"How did you know what I was thinking?"

"Please answer my question. Why would you want to devour a vital part of my anatomy? You are not hungry, I am certain of that. I can see into the kitchen, and I know that you've had a very fine breakfast provided by the same Lady who feeds me so well. You are most definitely not a bit hungry, so why would you want to do such an awful thing to me?"

"Why? Because I'm bored. In order to get your head into my mouth, I would have to capture you, and that would be an entertaining challenge."

"Can't you find a more constructive diversion than hunting?"

"It is not my nature to be constructive, madam—it is my nature to hunt. I am Classic Tabby," Kitten raised his nose proudly, "and my kind are born to hunt; we must hunt. The pursuit of prey is our *raison d'être*."

"Can you not overcome that savage animus, and strive to be civilized?"

"Savage? Nonsense! Hunters such as myself are quite civilized."

"No, sir; you are not civilized. You are a barbarian; blindly following your animal nature. Civilization is the transcendence of animalism."

"'The transcendence of animalism,' indeed!" Kitten snorted. "I believe what you are proposing is that I should become an unnatural cat."

"Not at all—I am proposing that you should become a better cat: a cat who thinks before he acts; a cat who considers all the consequences of his actions and cares about the welfare of others—a cat who looks at the big picture of life instead of seeking after nothing but his own interests."

"That is out of the question. Nature made me who I am. I would not presume to try to improve upon the perfection produced by that force which created me."

"When she created you, Nature provided your being with a set of many raw materials, including the genes of high intelligence for which Classic Tabbies are famous. I can see that you have, so far, chosen not to develop that promising intellect; showing only the tiniest flickers of its potentially vast power."

"There is no reason for me to develop my mind past the quite-adequate point it has already reached. All of my basic needs are taken care of here in this house, and I have conquered every challenge my environment has to offer. The only thing left for this mind of mine,"

Kitten's warm amber eyes suddenly took on a strange yellow glow, "is to fantasize about hunting you."

Dove's face suddenly became dead serious; her normally soft and gentle expression flashing into hard-focused intensity. Holding her head high, she slapped her wings furiously against her body.

"Flöbbertigôbbet!" the avian soprano sang; her voice leaping up into a fortissimo cry no ear could ignore. "Flöbbertigôbbet!"

A fearful quiet took hold in the garden as the chirping, warbling birds heard the alarm and fell silent. A moment later, a terrific bedlam of flapping wings ensued as all but Dove took flight and disappeared into the thick cover of the forest surrounding the great house.

Kitten's eyes lost their unnatural glow as he sat back in surprise. "Flöbbertigôbbet? What on earth is that? Is it some type of flibbertigibbet?"

"No, it is not. It is an entirely different creature, and it is not of earth, dear boy—it is a piece of animated darkness from the other world. To call it a living thing would be a lie, as it is antilife. Describing it as 'animated' is the best I can do within the limitations of ordinary language." Dove shuddered. "It's a horrible thing; an invader, and I see that it is here."

"From the 'other world,' eh? I didn't know there is another world." The small tiger looked a trifle distressed; thrown slightly off his intellectual balance by this reality-changing information.

"There is a great deal in life that a young one like you wouldn't know about," the bird said.

"Perhaps." The feline squinted as he considered this disturbing new data about his universe. "A piece of animated darkness is here, then?" Kitten looked round the room, then out at the garden. "I see no one but you. Where is it?"

"Where? It's lurking inside of you, young cat; festering like a quietly growing abscess. I saw it expose itself in your eyes just a moment ago."

"In me? I don't believe it." The tabby snarled in defiance; his white fangs contrasting against the pink of his open mouth's exposed interior. Bringing his ebony cat-lips close together again, he sniffed haughtily and shook his head. "There is nothing inside of me but myself."

"Excuse me, sir feline, but I saw the Flöbbertigôbbet quite clearly in your eyes. That unearthly glow—I've seen it once before, and know exactly what its source is. You have been touched by the Flöbbertigôbbet. One who has been touched by this powerful creature of evil becomes its servant."

"Servant? I am no one's servant! I am master of myself."

"You are wrong, sir. You have been brought into the service of the dark one, whose ways can be subtle. Stealth is one of the best ways for him to conquer. Without his victims being aware of the process, he acquires their persons and uses them to enlarge his army; going deep inside like the vile germ that he is to corrupt vulnerable hearts such as yours. He's the worst of invaders, conquering not territories but private psyches. The change in yours will probably start out in small alterations; barely noticeable at first. You might seem only a bit more moody than usual in the beginning. Have you developed a tendency to brood?"

Kitten blinked. "Well, yes."

11

"It isn't natural for a young, healthy cat to brood; especially when he is loved and well cared for, as you are."

"Well—you may say what you like, but I am certain that my moodiness comes about through nothing more malevolent than simple, ordinary boredom. Now, evil; I've heard about it before, but it's only a myth; a fairy tale intended to frighten naïve young kittens into obedience. There is no such thing as a creature of evil, therefore this Flöbbertigôbbet to which you refer cannot exist." The little tiger stamped his good front foot. "You are wrong, dear lady; quite wrong."

Dove sighed; a soft, quiet breath that barely stirred the air before her delicate beak. "I've learned from experience that there is often no point in talking to narrow-minded individuals about the existence of evil."

"You are calling me narrow-minded?"

"Yes, I am. You are a very young lad, probably not even a year old. I, however, have seen several summers come and go. But despite my certain wealth of experience, you have no respect for my advice. You are unwilling to open up your tight little mind and let in room for the idea that someone far older than yourself might know a bit more about life than you. In my book, that makes you narrow-minded."

Kitten looked past the bird and out at the garden. It was so beautiful there; curving areas of emerald-green lawn adorned by an abundance of colorful flowers planted in a natural style which allowed them to look at home at the edge of the old-growth forest that rose up at the far edge of the manicured grass. It all appeared serene and perfect; a paradise. "It's so lovely out there," the cat said, "and here in my house, everything is orderly and comfortable and sweet. I've seen no real evidence of this dark Flöbbertigôbbet thing; I have observed no clear signs of what one could call evil. How can I believe in something when I have no proof of its existence?"

"Do you believe that I, who have survived out here in a world filled with predators, am out of touch with reality, and therefore a font of unreliable information?"

The tabby considered this. Being a very bright young fellow, he didn't have to think about much of anything for long before he had it thoroughly figured out. His response came quickly. "I don't believe you are, exactly, out of touch with reality; ma'am, but perhaps your exposure to those who prey upon your kind has caused your powers of perception to become, somehow, out of whack, leading you to imagine evil where there is only natural order."

Dove shook her head; dismissing the feline's reply. "Do you watch your Lady's television with her?"

"Yes. I sit on her lap, and she strokes me while we look at wildlife and science programs. They're quite interesting. Did you know that I have relatives who are so large, they can chase down . . ."

The bird interrupted him with a wave of one wing. "Do you watch the news?"

"News? What's that?"

"A broadcast of current events." Dove inclined her head to the left, indicating where a large television crouched in a dark corner of the library. "Turn it on, please."

"I don't know how to do that."

"I do—I've watched through the window as your Lady operates the device. Press the red button at the bottom of the picture screen. That will turn on the set. Then push the blue button until you see a bright green number 'two' flash on the screen."

"Two?"

"Don't you know your numbers?"

"I know what they are. I can count pretty high, but I don't know how to read the symbols for numbers."

"Good heavens. All this time spent with humans, and you haven't learned . . ." Dove closed her eyes for a moment as she thought. "The Arabic numeral two is a bit hard to describe. However, it comes after one, which is simple. The number one is a straight up-and-down line, which usually has a tiny slanted line at its top and a small flat line at its very bottom. When you see that appear on the screen, press the blue button once and you will come to a twenty-four-hour news station."

"Okay." Kitten jumped off the stool and scampered across the room to the television. Turning it on as directed, he saw a field of white specks dancing on a black background, and in the upper left corner, the numeral '1' glowing in bright neon green. "This will be easy." The cat put his twisted left paw on the blue button and pressed lightly, and a '2' replaced the '1.' "Oh—that's a two!"

The tabby settled down on his haunches to examine the image that flashed onto the screen: the head and shoulders of a blonde woman standing in a makeshift hospital. The large tent was filled to capacity and more; overflowing with a multitude of patients.

"Today," the blonde intoned into her hand-held microphone, "more evidence of atrocities was found."

Kitten ran back to the window stool and leapt up onto it, his nose to the glass. "What's an atrocity?" he asked Dove.

"An extremely brutal, wicked, or cruel act," the bird replied. "Quite like what you wanted to do with my head."

"Hm." Kitten raced back to the television, where an open mass grave was being shown on the screen. The cat looked at the heaps of bodies and galloped back to the window. "Is all that the result of some kind of hunting?"

"It appears that a certain set of humans decided to hunt another set of humans because they hate them."

"I see." The tiny tiger returned to the television. He looked carefully at the flashing images of corpses, dazed children, and hysterical adults. It didn't seem right to him; it didn't seem natural. This wasn't like the hunting his big relatives carried out as they streaked across the African veldt in pursuit of dinner—this wasn't nature.

An elderly woman appeared on the screen. Tears streaming from her eyes, she began to lament in a foreign tongue. An unseen interpreter, speaking over the electronically softened voice of the weeping lady, began to tell the story of how this woman had been forced to watch as her husband and sons were shot to death.

Kitten began to feel sick. "How do I turn this off?" he shouted at the bird.

"Press the red button," Dove replied.

15

The feline pressed the button and the war vanished; leaving the library quiet and peaceful again. He jumped back onto the stool. "What I just saw was real?"

"Yes."

Kitten sat down and held his deformed paw close to his chest. This odd personal mannerism betrayed the fact that the cat was experiencing emotional distress. "In wanting to eat you when I wasn't hungry, I think I was no better than the people who shot that woman's family." The cat pressed his paw more tightly against the soft white fur of his chest. "I was bred to be a noble creature. I don't feel terribly noble right now."

"True nobility must be earned," Dove replied. "You can be born with the best blood nature has to offer, but without moral achievement, even the finest liquor of life is empty." The bird's eyes were downcast. "And when such ethically uncultivated blood has been infected by the Flöbbertigôbbet. . ." She sighed.

"Perhaps you are correct about the existence of this dark creature." Kitten put his paw down and stood at upright attention. "Can the thing be fought?"

"It has been a great many years since anyone known to us has sought to engage the beast in battle," Dove shook her head, "many, many years indeed. The stories have been told to me, handed down from mother to daughter for centuries. It's been, well; no one has gone through the Door since the year twelve ninety-three."

"The door? What door?"

"The Door which leads to where one must go in order to deal face to face, so to speak, with the Flöbbertigôbbet: the Door to the far place; the other world—it's behind you, in that room." The bird pointed a wing to indicate the library. "It's been there for as long as anyone can remember."

"And someone went through this Door in the thirteenth century? I didn't realize my Lady's house is so old."

"Parts of your mansion are so old that no one is certain of their true age. Now, this window we're talking through—it's practically new, compared to other parts of the dwelling; added in the early nineteenth century when an owner wanted more light in the library. But the mosaic and marble floor under that stool you're standing on—part of it was laid out by Romans in the first or second century. And some bits of the structure go back to a time before the Romans arrived. There are portions of your house's foundations which suggest the work of a culture so ancient that its identity is unknown—perhaps it was the same people who built the stone circles of Stonehenge, or perhaps it was another lost civilization: no one knows."

"I see. Well, this Door you refer to—it's not the oft-used one opening onto the corridor, obviously, since you said that no one's gone through it for several hundred years. I see no other door in the room. Are you certain it's in here?"

"Oh, yes; absolutely certain. Our histories are precisely memorized. While we don't know who created the Door, we do know where it is."

"Then kindly enlighten me."

"Those books on the bottom shelf to my right." Dove tilted her head in that direction. "Do you see the collection of volumes by Plato, Homer, and Aristotle?"

"Excuse me, ma'am—I can't read."

"Of course. Well, since you can't read the titles, you can go by the colors. That set of tan and black leather-bound books—do you see them?"

"Yes."

"The Door is behind them. To open it, one must step hard on the largest brown tile in the near right corner there," Dove pointed with her wing, "three times in quick succession. The portal then appears behind the classics collection."

"How big is the Door? Is it a wooden thing that opens on hinges, like all the other doors in the house?"

"I don't know how large it is or what it's made of. I've never seen it."

"You've never activated it yourself, not even to satisfy a simple curiosity?"

"I don't like to go inside houses unless there's a very good reason to do so. Being a creature of the open air, I find walled enclosures quite unpleasant. I do have neighbors who enter your house, though. Mice go in to sleep in the soft places; snakes like to enjoy the warmth of the Lady's various heating apparatuses on cold days; but those visitors do not toy with the Door. Such portals work two ways, you know, and it's hard to say who or what might come into our world if we were to activate the Door just to see what it looks like. It's best not to take the chance simply to satisfy one's curiosity."

"Still, I would think that an opening to another world would attract a great many adventurers. Why has no one gone through it since the thirteenth century?"

Dove shifted from one tiny foot to the other. The flat surface of the windowsill was not her usual sort of place to spend time—she preferred a nice thinnish twig on which to perch. "Well," the bird said, "the Lady's family has kept their knowledge of the doorway as a tightly held secret. And, uh; the last, um; fellow, or, whoever, well—whoever went through there in twelve ninety-three never came back."

"It was a man?"

"My family's histories hold no exact information regarding the gender or species of that individual."

"Well; let's call it a 'he.' Did he go through out of curiosity?"

"No. He went to fight the Flöbbertigôbbet. Everyone we know of who has gone through the Door has done so for the purpose of either meeting with or fighting the beast."

"Has anyone ever beaten the creature?"

Dove looked Kitten in the eye. "I don't truly know. According to our history, there is no record of anyone returning from the other side. We don't know what the place is like, or what happens to those who venture there."

"Yet you recommend that I go there to try to succeed where all others have apparently failed?"

"I recommended nothing. You asked me if the beast can be fought, and I gave you the only answer I have. You are free to choose not to go, and thereby accept your present fate: allowing the Flöbbertigôbbet to use you as its personal servant. That is what most of his victims do: submit, give in, et cetera."

Kitten's grey ears flipped back to lie flat against his skull for a highly irritated moment. "That would be a disgrace."

"That's correct." Dove nodded in agreement. "If I were in your situation, I would go through the Door."

"You would?"

"Yes. The fact that I am a creature of peace," the bird lifted her head proudly, "does not mean that I am a coward. I would rather die with dignity than be corrupted."

"You are an uncompromising lady."

"That is my nature. And I will make a promise to you. If you go through the Door, and fail to come back within a reasonable amount of time, I shall go in after you. I am beginning to like you. You're a grand little cat."

"Thank you, ma'am." Kitten bowed his head briefly. "Well! I do enjoy exploring the unknown, and I'm always looking for a good challenge; that's for certain. Even without the need to face this dreadful Flöbbertigôbbet, the prospect of going through the Door does provide me with the opportunity for a truly challenging adventure of exploration."

"One as young as yourself might view it as an adventure. Others, older and more cautious than you, would see it as a perilous quest: a quest where one doesn't know exactly what one is seeking."

"Can you describe the appearance of the Flöbbertigôbbet?"

"No. I have heard that it can alter its form at will, but that is only a rumor. I have no factual information as to his, or its, qualities when it is in its home in the other world, and I know only a small bit about its ways when it is here in our world. I don't even know if its actual self, if it has a true identity, is male or female." Dove sighed. "I would hate to think that the

Flöbbertigôbbet is a female. It's possible, I suppose, but I just don't like to think it." The bird tilted her head to one side; clearly perplexed by the subject at hand. "We are ignorant about so many things. I'm not even certain that the other side is the real home of the beast. Perhaps it's just a sort of prison from which it escapes now and then; perhaps?" She shook her head. "The situation is a great mystery."

"Perhaps I shall clear up that mystery, eh?"

"Perhaps."

"Well, there's no point in dilly-dallying about," the decisive young cat declared. "The Flöbbertigôbbet must be fought, and will be fought by me. I shall set about the doing of this without further delay. I'll see you after I defeat him!" Kitten jumped off the stool.

"I hope I will see you again," Dove whispered. "I do hope!" Turning from the glass, she flew up into the yew tree and perched on a high branch. She could have stayed at the window to watch Kitten as he activated the Door and went through its opening, but she could not bear to see him go. He was, as she had said, a grand little cat, and she feared for his life.

CHAPTER TWO

A Malevolent Mouse

Kitten was enveloped by an exceedingly unpleasant sensation: the feeling that he was being held in the mouth of something that didn't want to let him go as he tried to squeeze himself through the very tight-fitting Door. "What kind of nonsense is this?" the feline growled. With a push of his strong hind legs, he tried to jump clear of the weird, pain-inducing orifice that was expanding only slightly to allow his body through. "Darned unaccommodating, as doors go." The little tiger snarled as his fighting body was scraped by the apparent mastications of the rough something that was plainly reluctant to release him. But let go the rough something finally did. "Heads up!" the tabby cried as he cleared the opening; leaping out and down into a heavy mist that swirled like a thick ocean vapor below him.

Hitting a fog-shrouded surface which might have been ground, he landed lightly on all fours, then turned to look at what he had just jumped through. A solid stone wall, so high that he could not see its top, supported a sculptured human head that looked down at Kitten with a subtle hint of animation. Was there a spark of life in those cool marble eyes? The cat wasn't certain. As he stepped toward the wall for a closer look at the face, the dense fog swirling about him grew thicker, and he stopped in his tracks; unable to see.

In a flash, the all-encompassing mist went dark, and everything, even the feline adventurer, changed. The solid, safe qualities of ordinary life the tabby knew as comfortable everyday reality suddenly spun out and down into a deep, fearsome obscurity of utter blackness and zero physicality which had no equal in the world Kitten had known. The little cat was thoroughly shattered; absorbed into a dimension of fragmented silently screaming iciness that consisted of Nothing, Nothing, Nothing. The horror of this Nothing—what could be worse? Nothing to feel, nothing to see, nothing to hear, nothing to be: Nothing. The tiny tiger was part of this great Nothing: nonexisting in a complete void; chewed up and swallowed by Nothing.

Then, breaking into the empty agony of this horrible vacuum with a rumbling bereft of all possible comforting Somethingness came a roaring, deafening bedlam that went beyond any auditory sense the feline might have once had to occupy every iota of his newly dissolved yet somehow still extant being. This tumultuous clamor—a rushing of howling hurricane winds; a penetrating cacophony of thundering flash-flood waters—heralded the arrival of a terrifying unseeable Presence that wrapped itself around the flickering consciousness of the little tabby in terrible greeting and refused to let go. Caught within the empty mass of the great entity, Kitten was pulled deeper into the dimension of icy antimatter Nothingness.

Even with this Presence around him, the pitiful feline remnant was utterly alone; separated from Creation and himself. If he'd had a voice, he would have screamed from the pain of the complete and somehow chaotic isolation, but as was said before, he had, he was, Nothing, and so of course, had no voice. Even his memories were gone from him; the living treasure chest of what had once been his happy youthful mind was stripped bare and empty; leaving the poor lad essentially dead, and not only dead but a never-was never-lived dead. There was nothing left of Kitten but a solitary misery, void of any identity, and a horribly sensitized terror that he might be trapped forever in this ghastly dimension; a permanent prisoner of undiluted suffering.

The intensity of this unbearable horror increased with explosive growth until the infinitesimal bit that was left of Kitten's consciousness was rendered insane by fear. And then, from the great Nowhere Presence that surrounded him, a deep voice bellowed, "Enter!"

The awful Nothingness vanished; if Nothing can be said to disappear. Kitten was whole again; standing under a brilliant sun that illuminated a forest glade aglow with warmest life. His legs were shaking, and he began to hyperventilate in reaction to the dreadful stress he had just endured. "Breathe slowly," something at the back of his mind said to him. "Slow and easy."

The feline began to recover, and looked up to see that the oval patch of wild grass he stood upon was surrounded by trees with glittering leaves of flawless emerald. "Well! This is nice," the resilient young tiger remarked; the hideousness of his entrance into this strange place almost forgotten. "Yes, this is very nice indeed."

The tabby took a deep breath. Somehow the air seemed unlike the earthly atmosphere to which he was accustomed—or was the cat himself different? He felt changed, just a bit, though he could not ascertain in exactly what way, or be certain that he had really changed at all. Perhaps he was only imagining some subtle alteration in his being, perhaps—but this was no time to ponder unanswerable questions. Casting the matter aside, he decided to get on with a more pressing subject: his new environment.

Kitten took a careful step forward, feeling the unfamiliar sensation of grass under his feet. His life so far had been spent entirely indoors, and the pads of his pampered baby paws were uncalloused and quite sensitive; having been exposed to surfaces no rougher than highly polished wood and marble flooring occasionally interrupted by the soft pile of handwoven carpets.

The grass felt funny under his feet: a bit prickly, and damp; slightly bouncy. The fresh blades exuded a heady clean-perfume fragrance. Kitten put his nose down for a good sniff, and breathed in an extended draught. "Aaah—sweet."

Raising his head, he saw beside him a tall stalk of green topped with tiny yellow flowers. As a gentle breeze blew past, the stalk waved in the wind and nodded its golden head. The little tiger leapt up and slapped the cluster of blooms, and a few petals shook loose and fell to the ground. He scooped up a pawful of the bright canary petals and examined them. "Rather like what my Lady brings inside to put into bowls," the tabby murmured. As he gazed at the sunny bits that lay in his grey paw, they suddenly turned to deepest scarlet. Silver antennae erupted from the red petals as they formed themselves into the shapes of wings, joined into pairs and, having become sparkling ruby butterflies, the living jewels ascended into the air and perched amongst the emerald leaves of the nearby trees. "Well—not like my Lady's flowers at all!" Kitten declared.

The cat settled down onto his stomach to consider the situation. "This is a thoroughly new environment," he said to himself. "I should be careful. The trees and butterflies seem benign enough, though how a scientist would explain the manner in which gemstones can fly and grow on trees, I certainly don't know. This grass appears to be like the grass I've seen from my windows at home; however, since I've never touched or smelled English grass, or for that matter any outdoor plant before, I can't be absolutely certain that this is the same." Kitten pushed at a clump of the greenery with a tentative paw, and the blades of vegetation reacted by bending slightly under the pressure. "Hmm. Seems normal, I think."

He raised his eyes and looked around, observing that it was only the trees at the outer edges of the large patch of grass that bore emerald leaves. Beyond the edge of the bejewelled grove could be seen clumps of massive-trunked oaks with what appeared to be ordinary foliage. "Perhaps if I leave this spot and go to where the trees are apparently normal," Kitten said, "I will not have to deal with extraordinary occurrences such as flowers turning into butterflies. Being in a simple everyday outdoors will in itself be quite enough for a young house cat to handle at this time." Rising to his feet, he sprinted past the perimeter of the emerald grove; decelerating to a slow trot as he entered the forest of ancient oaks.

It smelled marvelous in the sheltering, shadowy wood. The fragrance sang out to Kitten in sweet tones of wildlife; the Wild Life. Vitality was everywhere: in worms who burped happily through nutrient-rich soil, in birds gathered in treetops conversing in beautiful song, in quiet brown rabbits nibbling happily at abundant grass, in gentle does who kissed their fawns under the watchful eyes of big-antlered bucks, in raccoons asleep in the cozy hollows of trees dreaming of what savory treats they might find in the course of the coming evening's forage.

Kitten smelled, heard, and felt the wild and unrestrained life that ebbed through the forest like a powerful ocean wave. As the heady current of élan vital washed over the little tiger, merging with his *Felis catus* blood, he began to breathe more quickly. His ears twitched at every tiny sound; his eyes grew big and bright. "I've never felt so alive!" he cried, and leapt high into the air for the sheer joy of it all.

As he came back down to land, his right front paw struck a small, sharp rock. No damage was done, but the moment of pain brought him back to himself, and he shook his head. "I must remember to be careful. This is a real forest. Here, there are creatures much larger and more dangerous than myself; predators who might look upon me as a tasty meal."

He regarded the oaks around him. The rough trunks of the forest's trees were extremely thick; obviously of very great age. "Judging from the imposing fatness of their mighty trunks, these trees are even older than my Lady's grand oaks, and hers have been growing for many centuries." Kitten was impressed. "As plants go, these are exceeding venerable." The collective mass of gigantic trunks and heavy-timbered branches surrounding the cat was so dense that, if it weren't for the scents and sounds of the living forest, the tiny tiger might have imagined himself to be inside a building, albeit one quite different from his Lady's house.

The tabby sat and observed the currents of life around him. On his right, a narrow stream of minute ants marched past; keeping in tight formation as their path traveled over the bumpy terrain of fallen leaves and broken twigs. On the feline's left, a shiny black beetle struggled to climb a gnarled oak root protruding from the forest floor. As the slow-moving insect attempted to scale a prominent knot bulging from the root's bent knee, he slipped and tumbled head over heels; landing upside down on the ground. Lying flat on his back, the creature waved his legs in the air; unable to right himself.

"Poor little beggar." Kitten sighed in sympathy. "I'm glad I'm not a beetle. One wrong move and there you are; stuck on your back with nowhere to go." Reaching out with his malformed yet dextrous left paw, the cat carefully flipped the bug over and onto its legs.

"Thank you, sir!" the insect croaked.

"Would you like a lift up to the top of the root?" Kitten inquired.

"No, thank you very much, sir. I must make my own way."

"Very well." The feline watched as the beetle started out on a new path, tackling a root with a gentler slope to it.

The bug moved too slowly to hold the attention of the young cat for long, and soon Kitten grew bored with his observation of the beetle's journey and turned

31

his eyes to the right, where the never-ending column of ants was still marching past him on its determined way to who knew where. The feline watched the line for a brief moment, then declared, "I didn't come to another world to watch insects go about their business. I am supposed to be on a great quest; seeking the Flöbbertigôbbet. But I don't know where to look, or even what to look for. Perhaps I should ask the beetle?" He turned to his left, but the *Coleopteran* was gone. "Well; I could try the ants." Placing his nose close to the marching army, he inquired in a soft voice, "Excuse me—do any of you know where I might find the Flöbbertigôbbet?" There was no response, so the cat asked again, in a louder voice this time, "Excuse me! Do any of you know where I might find the Flöbbertigôbbet?"

The ants did not break formation, pause, or answer; continuing on in their steady, silent stream. "Well!" Kitten snorted. "This is clearly a waste of time."

The tabby stepped out onto the forest floor. Picking his way through the tree-shaded layer of leaves and twigs, he kept an alert eye on his surroundings; watchful for threats or signs of anything more challenging than insects. Then, off to his right, he spotted distant flashes of light sparking through the heavy darkness of the wildwood, and a soft murmuring reached his sensitive ears. "Ah—what's that?" Curiosity overcame caution, and the feline broke into his fastest gallop; leaping high over fallen trees with a grace exceeding that of the well-bred equine hunters who jumped fences for Kitten's owner. "My Lady's Thoroughbreds got nothing on me!" the tiny tiger cried as he soared over a log three times his height, with plenty of room to spare between the obstacle and his flying feet. Landing on the forest floor so lightly that he barely disturbed the bed of dry leaves, he snorted with pride. "I'd like to see that big Irish bay my Lady loves so much clear a standard three times taller than him!" Kitten tossed his head in comic imitation of a spirited equine. "Aye; a horse may be a handy beast, but not one on earth can jump as finely as a cat."

Quite full of himself, he trotted toward the sparks of light that flashed through a space between two massive oak trunks. Squeezing his body through the narrow opening, he found himself standing on a moss-covered rock; one of many velvet-crowned stones huddled together on the shores of a sunlit stream bubbling with crystalline waters.

"Oooh . . . pretty." Kitten climbed over the jumble of small boulders to stand at the edge of the brook. Putting out a front foot, he dipped into the shimmering aqua pura and watched in delight as sparkling drops fell from his paw like so many tear-shaped liquid diamonds. "How wonderful! This is a nice place—I believe I shall stay a while." The feline chose a comfortable moss-cushioned flat spot whereupon he reclined and began to listen to the pleasantly relaxing sound of the stream that whooshed along past him. In no time at all, he started to feel sleepy. Curling into a tight ball on his sun-warmed bed of greenery, he closed his eyes in preparation for a catnap.

His attempt at slumber, however, was abruptly disturbed by something: a new sound, as constant as the murmur of the creek but much less soothing than the gentle song of the waters. Above the low tones of the brook moving over the rocky streambed could be heard an annoying chatter that seemed very much out of place in the primeval forest: a disharmonious yakking that made Kitten grind his back teeth in irritation. He tried to tune the noise out in order to get on with his nap, but the prattle was too high-pitched and aggravating to ignore.

The cat uncurled his furry form and stood up. After a moment of concentration, he ascertained that the source of the irritation was located in an area on his left, downhill from where he stood. Turning, he made his way across the rocks, leaping gracefully from one stone to the other; led by the ever-increasing volume of the noise.

When he came upon the source, he stopped; surprised. A mouse was seated upright on a raised section of broken twig; carrying on an animated and apparently one-way conversation as he held one hand tightly cupped to the side of his head. His back to the cat, the small creature shouted away to his lone little self like a natural-born lunatic. "My word!" the feline declared. "It's an insane mouse, making a hearty speech to no one but himself! Granted, I myself do tend to say a word or two into empty air at times, and in fact I do spew out my inner thoughts aloud quite a bit, but to pour out such an explosive stream of chatter in utter isolation—my goodness!"

The cat watched in amazement as the tiny mouse chortled, squeaked, and giggled away in a nonstop river of verbal noise; all the while keeping his right hand pressed to the side of his head as his left waved in extravagant gestures significant to no one but the rodent. Fascinated by the odd display, Kitten moved closer; sitting down a scant six inches from the minuscule creature's back. "Please—why are you talking to yourself?" the tabby inquired.

The mouse ignored the question, continuing to emit a frenzied flurry of verbiage. This went on for some time, and finally, Kitten lost his patience. With claws tensely extended, he reached out and tapped the rodent on top of its head; using a sharp talon to rap lightly against the creature's fur-covered skull. "Why are you talking to yourself?" the feline inquired once more.

There was a high-pitched shriek of surprise, and the mouse turned abruptly to look at what was behind him. As he spun about, Kitten saw a rectangular black object fall from the creature's hand onto the ground. The cat bowed down to peer at the object, and saw that it was a miniature cellphone.

The mouse, standing upright in a most unnatural fashion, put his hands on what passed in that position for rodent hips. "What is your problem?" he demanded of the feline. "That was a very important conversation you interrupted!"

"Oh . . . I'm sorry. Please—continue." Kitten watched as the mouse retrieved his tiny phone.   The small fellow addressed the device, listened for a moment, then punched furiously at the machine's keypad, over and over and over again; shaking his head and spitting in unbridled rodent rage. "What's the matter?" the tabby asked.

"My connection's gone, and I can't get it back!" the mouse screamed. Throwing his phone into the nearby stream, he stomped his foot. "It took me all morning to get that call through, and now a cat has to come along and mess things up. I ought to sue!"

"Sue? Sue who?"

"You!" The rodent's translucent ears were purple with fury. "I'll sue you!"

"Me? I'm a cat. How could I pay damages? I don't own anything."

"You don't own anything? Nonsense. Everyone owns things. In fact, to start out, you ought to give me your cellphone right now to replace the one you made me throw away. You made me get mad and toss my cell into the stream—you owe me a phone."

"I don't have a phone. What would I want with a cellular telephone? All my friends are close by," Kitten looked around at his strange new environment, "usually."

"How do you keep in touch with your broker? What if the market were to suddenly drop?"

"The market?" Kitten blinked, and the end of his tail twitched where it poked out from between his reclining back feet as he sat and stared at the bizarre little rodent. "The market, you say?"

"Yes, the market! I personally own ten thousand shares of PlanetTech, five thousand GeneMinip, and six thousand MicroDix. What stock do you own? Even one who professes to have nothing has investments in the market—everyone does."

"I am not everyone," Kitten replied.

"If you are not everyone, then you must be no one; a nobody."

Kitten's tail-end twitched a bit more violently. "You are most certainly wrong about that!" the feline declared. "I am somebody. I made a fine new friend today; a friend who says I am a grand little cat. She is a most noble dove, who has seen much of life. She thinks

I am so grand that she has promised to risk her life in order to save mine, should I fall into peril in this strange world. Dove is an ethical creature of honor who thinks I am somebody, and I value her opinion." The cat's ears switched flat against his head for an irritated moment. "I do not value the opinion of someone who makes a spectacle of himself; shrieking into an electronic device in an extremely undignified fashion and then throwing a tantrum when things go wrong."

The mouse smiled. The effect of this expression, biologically foreign to the face of a member of the genus *Mus*, was quite frightening when combined with the four-legged creature's habit of standing upright like a human. Kitten narrowed his eyes into half-shut slits in a failed attempt to hide the fact that he felt threatened by this weird animal; a being not much larger than one of the tabby's velvety-grey forepaws.

The rodent's grotesque smile grew wider and toothier as he gazed up at the feline. "You're afraid of me, aren't you? You know I'm very different from you, and you're afraid."

"Nonsense." Kitten's nervously blinking eyes betrayed the emptiness of his denial.

"If you want to be more like me, I can help you. I'm very important—I have top connections. You want a cellphone? I can get you the latest model on credit. It'll cost you next to nothing if you sign a contract with my carrier. Hey—you want to buy some stock? I'll loan you the money to buy a few shares, just to start you out." The mouse put one hand against his chest in the place where his heart possibly lay. The tabby, uncertain that this other-world creature had a heart at all, wondered if perhaps the little fellow's gesture was indicative of some type of stomach ailment. The rodent, not privy to the feline's personal thoughts, smiled earnestly. "I like you. You've got an honest face. We could be pals; good chums." The mouse grinned even more broadly, and his beady eyes glittered. "I can teach you to walk upright, so you'll look more important than your old friends. With a bit of work, you can be just like me. Whaddya say, dude?"

Kitten's right eye began to blink repeatedly as his left stayed warily open: a sign that the cat was dangerously irritated. "Be like you? I don't want to be like you! You're unnatural at best, and exceedingly shallow. Telling me I'm nobody because I don't own stocks: you're not only shallow, but rude. And you think that I would be stupid enough to mire myself in financial debt just so I could be your friend? Think again, Mouse!"

The rodent snorted. "Whatever!" Turning away, he walked off and disappeared behind a large rock. A moment later, there was the sound of an engine starting up, and a golden toy-sized sports-utility vehicle emerged from behind the big stone. The luxurious SUV's gilded-chrome accents glinted in the sun as the small but heavy machine made its way over the ground at high speed; churning up clouds of disturbed leaves and snapping fragile twigs under its fat little tires as it headed into the thick cover of the forest trees.

Kitten coughed, choking on the noxious haze of exhaust fumes left in the wake of the SUV. As the flashy vehicle vanished behind a big oak, the feline breathed a heavy sigh. "This is truly another world," he whispered. "And I'm not certain that I like every single bit of it."

The cat rose from his seated position and began to follow the edge of the bubbling stream; enjoying the feeling of warm sun on his back. His attention captured by the beauty of the sparkling waters, he failed to notice the stealthy figure at the edge of the wood. Hiding in the deep shadows cast by the ancient trees, the creature was following Kitten's progress as the feline made his way forward.

CHAPTER THREE

The Alpha She-Wolf

The little tiger had been making his way along the edge of the brook forever; at least, it seemed that way to him. The soft pads of his pampered feet, unaccustomed to transit over rough stones and prickly forest debris, were starting to throb. Pausing to rest, the cat looked at the stream bubbling past. "That water is cool, and my feet are hot. I believe a dip would be most beneficial to me." Stepping into a shallow area at the creek's edge, he let the refreshing currents soothe his unhappy paws. Relief from the pain was almost immediate, and Kitten let out an exuberant meow. "That feels so good!" he cried.

As the tabby stood in the healing waters, enjoying the comfort offered by the crystalline stream, he heard a mournful wail. Looking about, Kitten saw off to his left a pretty little goldfinch perched atop a purple-flowered clump of thistle. The feline called out to the bright-colored bird. "Are you all right?"

The finch lifted her black-spotted wings and soared into the air. Circling over the cat in up-and-down roller-coaster curves, she poured out a wordless song in tones that expressed the gravest lamentation.

Kitten watched as the bird circled overhead. "Please, ma'am; whatever is the matter?" he asked.

The airborne singer spiraled downwards and landed on a boulder at the edge of the creek. "The worst that can happen to anyone has happened to me!" she cried, the agony in her voice a heartbreaking sound indeed. The finch began to tear at her feathers, scattering bits of plumage onto the ground.

"Stop it!" Kitten jumped out of the stream and ran to the bird. "You mustn't hurt yourself like that!"

"I cannot bear it; I cannot bear it!" Hiding her head under an outstretched wing, the goldfinch began to tremble.

"Please, dear lady—tell me what's wrong. Perhaps I can help."

The bird's head came out of hiding, and she looked the tabby directly in the eye. "The mongoose; the horrible mongoose—he killed my babies: all of them!"

"No!"

"I saw him, sir! I was flying back to my nest, carrying food for my children. When I got within sight of home, I saw that the nest was empty, and the vile mongoose was standing on the ground below it. He was smiling—there was blood on his murderous lips and my babies' feathers on his dreadful paws!" The finch's tremors grew more violent, and she began to gasp for breath.

"Oh, no." The cat sat back on his haunches. "Oh, no." He thought of saying, 'I'm sorry,' but felt such words of sympathy would sound woefully inadequate. Not knowing what would be proper behavior in such a terrible situation, the tabby decided to do what seemed the best thing to him: he stepped forward and began to gently lick the bird's face. This was what his mother had done for him during unhappy times, and it had always been a comfort. When his well-formed brothers and sisters cruelly teased the little tiger about his funny front paw and crooked spine, as they were wont to do far too often, Mama would lick the tiny feline to let him know that he was loved. It was the best gesture of kindness Kitten knew, so he offered it.

The goldfinch sat quietly as the cat groomed her cheeks and forehead with his pink tongue. Her trembling gradually lessened, and she began to appear calmer. "Thank you, sir," she finally said. "I believe I have regained possession of myself; at least to some small degree."

The tabby stepped back and looked at the bird. "Where is your mate?" he inquired. "Do you have a spouse who can help you get through this tragedy?"

"No. My mate disappeared some time ago. I don't know what became of him."

"I see." Kitten observed the finch, who seemed frozen somehow; alive yet not alive. Her grief must have changed itself into another form, the feline decided; going from raw hysteria into cold numbness. "There must be something I can do for you, ma'am. May I protect you as you make your way home?"

"I will not go home again. There is no longer anything there for me." The goldfinch fixed her eyes on the tabby. "But there is something you can do to help me."

"I am at your disposal. Speak, and it shall be done."

"I want you to kill the mongoose."

"Oh." The cat sat down on a rock, surprised. "Oh."

"Is that a problem?"

Kitten squirmed a bit. "Well, yes."

"Why? Are you afraid?"

"Fear is not the problem, though judging from what I've seen on televised nature programs, in a fight with a mongoose I might very well lose my life. If the animal is similar to a Spanish mongoose, otherwise known as *Ichneumon*, its size would exceed mine. And since any mongoose's agility and quick eye enable it to overcome the most ferocious types of venomous snakes, and as its stiff hair and thick skin give it an unfair battle advantage over a soft-coated, tender fellow like me, well; yes, there's a very good chance indeed that I would perish if I attempted to fight a mongoose to the death. But my demise is not the point, since I am not afraid to die. No, fear is not the problem."

"What is the problem?"

"The plan of me deliberately trying to kill another animal: that's the problem. I don't like the idea of the intent to kill."

"You're a cat. Killing is nothing more than sport for you, is it not?"

"Once, it was; but that attitude of mine was changed this morning. A friend showed me one of the faces of evil, and how in that one particular form it kills for power and savage pleasure. I don't like that face, and will not wear it willingly."

"I'm not asking you to kill for pleasure and power. I'm asking you to avenge the deaths of my children. Such an act would be honorable, not evil."

Kitten considered the bird's statement for a short moment before he spoke, mentally calculating the aspects of the problem with his usual rapid-fire speed. "I don't believe that any killing can be considered honorable, ma'am; no matter what the motive. Killing appears, at certain times, to be necessary for survival. But even if one is pushed to kill by certain circumstances, it seems to me that the taking of life can never be considered an act of integrity or honor—at best, it is one sometimes born of need: a necessary evil, so to speak. Vengeance is not a necessity."

"Vengeance is not necessary? How can you say that? There's a killer at large in the forest, preying on helpless children! He must be stopped!"

"You didn't ask me to restrain a murderer—you asked me to carry out an act of deadly revenge. That would be illegal, in my world. To do this right, first we have to find a constable who can capture the suspect, then there has to be a trial to prove that the mongoose did indeed take the lives of your children, and after that, the court would choose the correct punishment for the crime. I have heard my Lady discuss such matters, and this is the correct way. For me to run off and kill the mongoose at your request: that would be the wrong way. I'm sorry, ma'am. I know you are in great and terrible pain, but I won't kill for you."

"You are a coward!"

"I am not a coward, ma'am. I am simply striving to behave in a civilized fashion."

Kitten remembered the mass graves he had seen on the televised news, and the destructive runaway emotion that had no doubt led to the carnage. He could see it now—if he were to kill the mongoose, the mongoose's relatives would come after him and the goldfinch, and if one of them were to die, there would be a need for more revenge, with friends and relatives called in from all sides. There would be a war in the forest; with each party enacting revenge on the other, over and over and over again in a relentless bloodbath. And then, of course, there was the matter of the killing itself: stripped clean of all the possible physical consequences, such an act of violence would simply be morally erroneous. The feline had changed—whether it was because of Dove's interaction with him, or the subtle alteration that had seemed to occur as the tabby went through the Door, he didn't know, but Kitten had become a different cat. The hunting which had once seemed like the purest feline fun was now thoroughly abhorrent to the little tiger.

Pushing aside the feelings of sympathy and outrage aroused in him by the bird's plight, Kitten continued on the path he had chosen. "I'm very sorry, dear goldfinch, that you have been so grievously wronged, but I will not kill for you or anyone else. That is my final word on the matter."

"Whatever!" the bird snapped, a peevish tone in her voice. Erupting into furious wing-snapping flight, the tiny creature jetted into the forest; gone from sight in a quick second.

"'Whatever'," the tabby mused, nibbling absently at a front paw. "That's exactly what the mouse said after I insulted him, which seemed suitable. But I must say; such a response doesn't seem at all appropriate for a well-spoken grieving mother. One would think, well; it just doesn't seem right." The cat shook his head. "This place is truly and exceeding strange," he said, "but I'll worry about that later. For now, I'm long overdue for a nap." In typical feline fashion, he flopped down onto his side, stretched out his tired little body, and fell fast asleep.

A pair of amber eyes had observed Kitten's interchange with the goldfinch, and watched from a discreet distance as the exhausted cat fell deep into sleep; his limbs twitching faintly as he entered the dream state. That stealthy form, one which had been shadowing the tabby since he first arrived in the emerald grove, emerged now from within the cover of the forest. Creeping forward on silent feet, it approached the slumbering feline.

The she-wolf was an imposing example of the *Canidæ* family: the root creature from whom came forth that loyal best friend of man—the family dog. But this was no one's obedient servant; that fact was made crystal-clear by one direct look from her black-rimmed eyes. This was a creature who could love, certainly, but she chose whom she loved and on what terms she might express that affection. She was a leader, not a follower.

The canid was large; larger than someone from our world might expect a female wolf to be. Despite her size, she seemed almost weightless; an illusion given by a graceful fitness that allowed her to move over the rough terrain of the wild forest as effortlessly as a ballerina might dance across the polished boards of a stage. In reality, the lady was solid and substantial. Under a beautiful coat brilliantly marked by shades of grey, white, silver, and black was a tough fighter's body whose total mass equalled that of a large, well-built man.

Putting her nose close to Kitten, she sniffed the slumbering fellow from end to end and performed a brief visual inspection of his malformed paw and tail.

More time was spent looking over the soft pads of the feline's house-cat feet; their painful scrapes easy to see.

Her examination finished, the wolf turned and trotted over the rocks to the stream. Going knee-deep into the currents of the brook, she stood motionless; staring down into the rushing water with an intense gaze. A few moments later, a shimmering trout jumped up into the air directly below the canid's nose, and she caught the rainbow-hued creature in her jaws; seizing it with a lightning-quick crush that brought an immediate end to the catch's life.

Carrying the trout in her mouth, *Canis lupus* left the creek and returned to the sleeping cat. After placing the fish on a mossy stone near the tabby, the wolf vanished into the forest.

Kitten opened his eyes reluctantly, roused by a gust of wind that had reached through his fur to prod him into wakefulness. "Oh—that was such a lovely dream! I was home, and my Lady was feeding me lunch." He sighed with deepest longing. "Tasty kippers and tender mouthfuls of Stilton cheese; I would surely enjoy that right now. I'm so hungry!" Raising his head, he watched the stream rush past; its waters glistening in the low-angled sunlight of late afternoon. "I must have been asleep for a very long time—the morning is lost, and even midday has come and gone. But my dreams were so cozy, I hated to leave them: my Lady stroking me and talking in her soft sweet voice; telling me how I'm her little darling. She loves me, and I miss her. Nobody loves me here; they just try to sell me things on credit or ask me to commit crimes. This is an awful place! I want to go home!" Kitten sniffed. "Cats aren't supposed to cry, but I believe I shall if one more creature tries to entangle me in debt or felonious acts." The feline sniffed again. "What's that I smell?"

Turning his head, he saw the trout that had been deposited on a rock behind him. "That's curious: a fish lying in a place where it has no business." The cat rose and examined the specimen. "Well, it's quite dead. I hope it will be all right if I eat it—I'm absolutely famished."

The little tiger squatted down on all fours and began to consume the trout; carefully separating the flesh from the fragile skeleton in the manner he had learned from watching his Lady and her cooking staff as they deboned fish for safe eating by the tabby, though of course, the feline had to make do without the aid of a sharp kitchen knife. "This isn't bad," Kitten said, swallowing the first bite. "I prefer the cooked version, but if one is starving from hard exercise and a long nap, this isn't bad at all."

In a little while, he had finished every edible bit of the fish. "I feel better now—I believe I shall not weep like a baby if I meet another foe in friendly clothing." He looked across the stream to the other side, where a low-set sun was sinking behind the dense mass of the

49

forest. "That must be the west, if they have such planetary orbits and whatnot in this world. I do need to establish a sense of direction if I'm ever to find my way back home again. Let's see . . ." Kitten looked upstream, and his heart sank. "Oh, no. I remember running through the woods when I saw the light sparkling on the brook, but I don't recall the exact spot where I first came to the water, or the precise location of the emerald grove. How will I ever find my way back to the Door? Oh, no—I am lost; quite lost."

The sturdy little cat mustered his courage and stood proudly upright. "Well—that's that; no point in fretting over something I can't change. Night will be falling soon, and a small fellow like me can't be found hanging about on the shores of a stream where nocturnal predators will surely come to drink and hunt. I must find a safe place to hide until morning. Perhaps a cave; yes, I shall search for a cave."

Kitten looked at the stream, reluctant to leave the shimmering ribbon which had become something of a companion to him; always there, steady and reliable. "If I cannot locate you again, dear brook, it will likely be quite impossible for me to find my way back to the Door, and to home. I hope I'm not making a mistake." The feline bowed his head. "I must go—death will come to me if I linger here."

The little tiger turned and bolted into the cover of the forest before he could lose his resolve. Stopping just inside its wooded border, he looked at the oaks around him. "Surely there must be some distinguishing features I can memorize which will allow me to find my way back to this place, and to the stream again." But all the trees looked very much the same: huge, gnarled, dark, and unfriendly. "Well; perhaps if I become desperate enough, my instincts will kick in and allow me to return here and then get back to my home, somehow. I am, after all, a feline, and we are known for our ability to find our way when we must." Head held high, the cat strutted off through the wildwood with an air of mock confidence, which seemed better to him than no confidence at all.

Twilight was much too short in this world; expressing itself in what seemed only a brief moment of sweet pale-purple light that came and went in a tantalizing flash. As the lavender glow vanished, darkest night swallowed the forest in a sudden voracious bite; making it cry out in noises far colder than those of the warm pleasant morn: sounds dreadfully opposite to the vital nature of the bird song and happy chatter that had filled the wood earlier in the day. The force that expressed itself now was redolent of hunger, and fear, and longing: growlings and whimpers punctuated by the staccato of scrabbling feet; whinings and whirrings that bespoke pursuit and flight; shrill screams articulating the futile desperation that comes before a violent end.

The fur along Kitten's spine rose up. Such terrors were utterly foreign to the gentle experience of a beloved house pet. In this wild, hungry place each and every bush could conceal a lurking predatory animal; a lion, perhaps, who would think nothing of making the young cat into its evening meal. In his Lady's house, the tabby had been the king of beasts; the only beast, if truth be told, aside from an occasional mouse who might cross his path and instantly flee at the sight of the tiny tiger. Excepting his Lady's water atomizer,

Kitten had found nothing to fear in his fine house. But this place: this wild, hungry place where a small Shorthair counted as no more than a tasty dish; this wild, hungry place where rustlings and crunches seemed not mere noises but harbingers of impending death—this wild, hungry place was dreadful.

The little feline was frightened out of his wits, and wanted nothing more than a hole in which to hide. Crouching down low to make himself less visible, he glanced about; looking for a fallen log to dart under. He could see nothing but useless twigs and shallow beds of dry leaves, and began to panic.

Suddenly, out of nowhere, there came a loud thumping crash behind Kitten, and he flew straight up into an airborne half-pirouette. As he landed and saw what had made the noise, the cat let out a piercing howl of mind-wrenching horror.

It was a Thing normally seen only in one's worst nightmares. Grey it was, and shiny with foul-smelling slime. Mud-brown eyes glowed with an ugly yellow light that had no place in nature, and a gaping loose-lipped maw dripped horrid foaming saliva carrying shredded remnants of the Thing's last meal: a repast which had once been a living creature; a being who sadly did not die until a grotesquely long while after it was imprisoned within the Thing's huge mouth.

Lumpy grey *Homo sapiens* hands armed with ragged black talons reached out to Kitten, and he did a quick turn and leapt forward. The Thing kept up with the feline, moving ahead on two thick stumps which might have been legs, and let out a moist, horrible laugh that sounded far too much like an act of gastrointestinal expulsion.

Kitten, overtaken by blind terror, suddenly froze in his tracks and screamed from his deepest gut. He didn't know he could scream, and in his short life had experienced no reason to think otherwise. But an agent of Death now loomed near him, and it wasn't a noble dealer of eternal rest—it was a disgusting filthy killing Thing that emanated joyous cruelty: a dæmon from hell that had come into the forest to exercise unnatural ways; fulfilling a diabolic need to inflict pain and snuff out life. It was the most hideous Thing imaginable, so Kitten screamed, and screamed, and screamed.

A set of dirty talons reached out to the terrified cat's fear-rigid form. An inch from the tabby, the filthy claws suddenly stopped; then withdrew. The Thing paused, turning its ugly eyes to the feline's right.

The she-wolf had appeared at the tiny tiger's side in flat-out battle stance: amber eyes ablaze with cold fire, long sharp fangs of purest white bared to gum-showing exposure. Her slavering lips were aquiver with ominous portent as the canid's throat sent forth a marrow-freezing growl of menace no creature of nature could fail to respect. Even the Thing, as far outside nature as it was, could not fully ignore the power of this threat. Peering at the wolf with muddy eyes, it gave a moment's dull consideration to her warning. A brief second later, it spit forth another retch of vomit-like laughter. Exposing the limitless depths of its reservoir of stupidity, the Thing reached for Kitten, who was still screaming in blind panic.

The wolf wasted no time. Though only half the size of the Thing, she sprang into action; leaping forward and clamping her powerful jaws onto the slimy hand before it could snatch the feline. The canid's deadly fangs dug into the monstrous flesh, and a mucous green liquid leaked out. The Thing snorted and pulled back, shaking its brutish low-browed head in pain. It roared and tried to extricate its hand from the wolf's jaws, but *Canis lupus* held on tight. The greater the effort the Thing put forth in its attempts to free itself, the more the wolf clamped down; digging her teeth in with such ferocity that they separated the joints of the heavy bones in the creature's hand.

The Thing began to wail, pouring out a series of nasty gurgling sounds. The wolf understood the dreadful noises erupting from the creature's throat. "Monster!" she grunted through the tightly clenched jaws that continued to grip the beast's hand. "Do you give up?"

The Thing whimpered and nodded its head.

"Do you promise . . ." Wolf growled in disgust as the creature's vile green blood ran onto her tongue, "do you promise to leave the small one alone?"

The Thing nodded again.

"Very well." Wolf relaxed her jaws, and the wounded hand withdrew from her mouth. The Thing backed a safe step away from the pair before him: the now-silent Kitten, who had apparently fainted, and the canid, who had just spit out a thick glob of foul monster-blood. "If you know what is good for you," the she-wolf snarled, "you will keep your promise. I am more powerful than one as dull-witted as yourself might think."

The Thing smiled, showing broken yellow teeth. "Stupid female!" it laughed. "Do you truly believe you can win a real fight against me? Do you have any idea how many relatives I have?" The dæmon chortled in

54

that awful retching way it had. "You mangled my hand, but it will heal very quickly. And when it does, we will find you, and we'll have you and your little kitten there cooked up for a very nice meal."

"Don't waste your energy pretending to be so fine that you would take the time and trouble to cook your victims," Wolf snarled, "or even kill them before you eat. I know better."

"If you're familiar enough with my kind that you know our dining habits, then you must know that you've made a big mistake. You should have let me have the cat. I am not one to make an enemy of."

"We were enemies before we ever met, Monster— that is the way of things. And as I said before, I am more powerful than you might think. It would be best for you if you kept your word."

"That's a laugh." A grotesque smile showing on its ugly mouth, the Thing turned away and lumbered off into the darkness.

Wolf looked down at Kitten's pitiful form. The horrible event had been far too much for the tiny tiger, and his overloaded mind had shut down; causing him to pass out cold on the ground. His new friend pushed gently at his head with her black nose, but he failed to react. "Poor little fellow," she whispered, "I must get him to a safe, quiet place." Using her mouth, she picked up the feline in the same careful way she had lifted her pups when they were small.

She trotted forward with the unconscious tabby hanging from her jaws; his limp legs swaying in rhythm with her steps. It was easy for *Canis lupus* to see clearly in the near-total darkness of a forest night, and she stepped smoothly through the tangle of trees and underbrush; her practiced feet flowing gracefully over the rough terrain with a wild-born ability that was outright magic.

The canid came to an open area and paused to look around. A curving crescent moon, a fat sliver of pale white, could be seen in the star-spotted dome of night sky overhead; sending a silvery illumination down into the glade. Scanning the black-shadowed clearing, the wolf's sharp eyes spotted a skinny creature taking his ease in a bed of dry leaves. The coyote, seeing the lady stride toward him, jumped up to stand at attention. "Ma'am!" He raised a front foot in something like a salute.

Wolf deposited the unconscious bundle of cat fur on the ground; gently setting him down atop a soft pile of foliage. "First Coyote!" She flashed a forepaw in response to the salute and assumed a position of rest; lying in a Sphinx-like position with Kitten between her front feet. "Relax, son."

The coyote seated himself on his haunches and looked down at the miniature silver tiger. "Who have you got there, ma'am?"

"An ambitious young friend in need of assistance," Wolf replied. "He's come here from the other world, apparently with the intention of finding the Flöbbertigôbbet. I don't know why he wants to find the Beast, but he was asking after its location."

"I see."

"He's a house cat—his paw pads are scraped and irritated by their first contact with natural ground. Today was his first day outside—I overheard him talking to himself about the fact that he'd never encountered outdoor plants before—and I'm fairly certain he is English. He seems like an American in some ways, but still; yes, I believe he's from England. Though his style with individual words is occasionally difficult to categorize, he has something of an English intonation to his speech."

"Oh, my. An English house cat—a mere babe— loose in our forest! He is in need of assistance, isn't he?"

"Yes. I doubt that he would have been willing to do what was necessary to feed himself until he was so close to starvation that he'd have been too weak to hunt effectively. Judging from what I observed, he'd be likely to get lost in a battle with his private conscience over whether or not he should kill for his supper. I expect he would try to survive on wild grasses if left to his own devices, and might even drown in an ethical dilemma over whether or not it would be right to take the life of a plant. I've seen, however, that when he's hungry, he'll eat a fish that someone else has killed."

"He's idealistic but practical, then."

"Yes." Wolf tilted her head to one side as she looked down at the inert form of the tabby. "The little one seems quite brave, though he fell apart when he met one of the grey monsters. That's why he's unconscious now—he fainted."

"That's understandable. They certainly scare me. If my mother hadn't taught me about them when I was very young, and I had suddenly come upon one by surprise—good heavens; I'd have fainted, too."

"I stopped the grey from eating this kitten, and he's vowed to come back after me." The wolf squinted in disgust. "He said he'll bring his family with him."

"Not a problem, ma'am. You know your army will fight with you. Not one of your soldiers will abandon their General when she's in need."

"Thank you, First Coyote—I know I can trust my troops." The canid gazed down at the tiny bundle of fur that lay in a limp pile between her forelegs. "It makes me angry that the monster frightened this child so terribly, and I become even more furious when I think that he most likely ran off to kill someone else; someone who wasn't ready to go yet. The cruel deaths the greys deal out for the sheer pleasure of killing: how long will it keep going on?" Wolf shook her head. "Yesterday was a bad day, friend. I kept running into creatures who say our world has to be this way because it has always been this way—evil has been here as far back as anyone can remember, so evil must have always existed and therefore will forever be with us as a supposedly ineradicable presence. I kept meeting those who preach that evil cannot be eliminated and we shouldn't try to fight it. Avoid it, yes; they say we should do that, but fight it? No, no; we aren't supposed to try to overcome evil because it's a hopeless waste of energy. What nonsense! Certainly the Flöbbertigôbbet gives the impression of being too powerful to conquer, but how can one not try? How can so many skulk through life never even daring to hope for a world where evil has been vanquished?" Wolf's head began to droop, as though the physical weight of it was too much to bear. After taking a long, deep breath, she resumed her statement. "I can understand why they don't want to personally go into battle against the Flöbbertigôbbet; I can appreciate their fear of such a dangerous confrontation; but why, oh why must they tell others that we shouldn't even try to fight?" There was desperation in the canid's voice, betraying the strain she had been under for some time.

First Coyote, alarmed by this unusual display of what seemed a weakness in the military officer before him, attempted to encourage her. "Your bravery is the reason you're our General, ma'am. You will never knuckle under to the advice of the fearful; no matter how large their number may be. I know there seems to be an awful lot of such weaklings, but they are in the minority, you know. Like all cowards, they travel in packs, and that makes them seem more numerous than they truly are."

"But I must admit," Wolf closed her eyes and sighed wearily, "sometimes it's so hard, First Coyote; so very, very hard; to not knuckle under. When scores of creatures band together to tell me that I'm wrong; that I'm unrealistic." She bowed her head down low. "Sometimes I just get very tired."

"When did you last sleep?"

"It's been a while." The General's eyelids began to droop. "I was up yesterday and all through the night with business, then I tracked the kitten all day today and watched out for him as he slept. He's special, somehow." She paused a moment to rub her eyes with one forepaw, then looked down at the tabby. "The little one needed me."

"I'm sure he did, ma'am, but you are mortal, after all, and you must sleep. I respectfully suggest that you retire to your den immediately. No one will trouble you —I'll stand guard with my brothers."

"Thank you, son. That's a good idea." Wolf rose to
her feet, picked Kitten up with her mouth and trotted
into the woods; followed by the coyote.

The den was not far from the glade, and the travelers arrived within a few minutes. The General's enclosure was a cozy space at the base of a giant oak, hidden inside a tangle of closely interwoven roots and fallen branches. The small lair's hard earth floor was cushioned by a layer of leaves mixed with winter fur shed by the wolf during the many springs she had lived and raised pups there. It had been several years since she had given birth to a litter, and it felt good to have a small one in her charge again. Carefully laying the limp kitten down upon the soft natural carpet of the den, the canid's eyes brightened as she looked fondly at the tiny silver tiger. "He's extremely cute, isn't he?"

"He's very attractive, ma'am. I like the bold dark stripes that stand out in such a fine pattern on his legs, and those white whiskers are delightful. I have yet to see his eyes, however. When do you think he'll wake up?"

"In time; in time." The wolf reclined on her bedding, bending her legs protectively about the unconscious feline. "He's had a very rough day; coming into the wild for the first time, then having to deal with two agents of the Flöbbertigôbbet, and of course that awful encounter with the grey. He probably thought I was dangerous, too. In his world, things are different. As you know, wild creatures there can't choose their meals as agreeably as we can—where the kitten comes from, a wolf would likely have been forced to make this tiny one into dinner. Yes, the little thing's had a very bad day, and will need a good long sleep so his mind can sort things out."

"He does need a good night's rest, poor fellow. Well; I'll call my brothers." First Coyote sat down and focused his gaze straight ahead onto the rough wall of the den. It was clear that he wasn't actually looking at the wall, but had turned his attention inside himself. He concentrated for a few moments, then breathed out a quiet sigh. "They're not far off; they should be here almost immediately. I asked them to make good time."

"Thank you." Wolf closed her eyes, unable to stay awake any longer.

The coyote went to the entrance of the lair and stationed himself in the opening. A few seconds later, a pair of skinny creatures nearly identical to him came bounding to his side and took up their posts. "You two can stay awake all night?" First Coyote asked. "The General needs solid protection right now."

"We know—we've seen the increase in hostile activity. The enemy is everywhere—they started showing themselves in force a few hours ago. What's happening, anyway?" The smaller of the new arrivals tilted his narrow head to one side.

"I don't know what's happening, exactly, but I do know we have a visitor—look at that little one there." First Coyote turned and pointed a forepaw, indicating the slumbering Kitten. "The General said he's come from the other world to find the Flöbbertigôbbet."

"Another one? There are so many coming through the Doors these past few years."

"Yes, there are. Almost seems like an exodus at times."

"Why does he want to find the adversary? Did he come to fight the beast or join him?"

"We don't know for certain. There's been no opportunity to question him yet. But Wolf said she can tell that the cat is an idealistic creature, so it's unlikely that he wants to join the enemy."

"Look at how the General's bent her legs about him as though he's one of her pups," the third coyote observed. "She's clearly taken a great liking to him."

"Yes."

"Wolf never judges a character wrongly. If she likes him, he must be a good chap."

"I expect you're right." First Coyote nodded. "But keep quiet now; the lady needs her rest."

"Yes, sir!" the two brothers whispered in unison. Turning their eyes to the forest, the trio settled down for a long night's watch.

Kitten purred blissfully and pushed his pink little nose deeper into the soft stomach-fur that had kept him warm through the night. "Mommy," he murmured. "Mommy." His head began to clear itself of the heavy fog of sleep, and the cat blinked in alarm. "Wait a minute: Mama's gone. I left her behind when I was weaned and relocated to England. Oh—and I'm not even in the same world as England anymore! Who is this soft-stomach-fur person?" The tabby pulled away from the comforting coat. Seeing the face of the sleeping wolf, he started to his feet; ready to flee. The main exit, however, was blocked by the three guards: First Coyote recumbent in the center of the egress; his two brothers standing at sentinel duty on either side of him.

Kitten backed away from the slumbering canid and looked for an alternative exit. Glancing around, he spotted a narrow space between two clumps of branches through which shone a beam of early morning light. In order to reach that aperture of escape, however, he would have to pass close by the face of the wolf. "Don't have much choice," the feline muttered. He took a careful step forward, followed by another, and another.

"Ma'am!" a coyote called out. "Cat's awake!"

The General opened her eyes and rose up onto her forelegs just as Kitten was passing before her nose. The little tiger froze in his tracks, stood his ground as bravely as he could, and let out a tiny yet quite fierce snarl.

"Cat," Wolf said gently, "I'm your friend. There's no need for antagonistic noises."

"You're a wolf!" The cat hissed, trying to conceal his terror with a show of bravado. "I know about your kind. You eat little fellows like me!"

"You're not at home any longer, friend. Things are different here." The General put her nose close to the tabby's face. "Do you think I'd have let you spend the night curled up by me if I intended to make a meal of you? Such an act would be perverse indeed!"

Kitten flopped down on his belly in an attitude of reluctant submission. "This is a perverse world, Madame Wolf." He looked up into the canid's eyes. "I have met twisted creatures here: an upright-walking mouse who chatters on a cellphone and drives a sports utility vehicle; a pretty little finch who tried to induce me to commit a murderous crime; a slimy grey thing that smelled foul and laughed in the most disgusting way. It would not surprise me to meet someone who would treat me with kind affection as a prelude to eating me."

"You didn't see that I was defending you from the grey monster, then?"

"No. I thought the two of you were fighting over dinner, and I was the meal."

"Since your mind chose a bad time to shut down, falling into unconsciousness before you had a chance to see what I'm made of, I suspected you might form a bad impression of me. I know a thing or two about your world."

"How did you know I'm not from here?"

"I saw you appear in the emerald grove. That is one of the usual points of entry for foreigners; for those from your world. I've been following you since then."

"Do you know how I can get back there?"

"You want to go home already? You've just barely arrived."

"I don't like it here—I don't like it one bit." Kitten's face was as tragic as a cat's can be: ears flattened; eyes narrowed. "Everything is hostile."

"I'm not hostile, and neither are the three coyotes there. Give us a chance before you run back home."

"Home . . ." Kitten thought of his Lady and the sweet safety of her house. He bit his lower lip and sniffed. "I want to go home!"

"All right—I can show you the way back to the emerald grove, if you insist," Wolf said, "but before we go, please tell me why you came here. I overheard you inquiring about the location of the Flöbbertigôbbet. Why were you seeking him?"

"It's a him, then?"

"Well, yes; most of the time. Why did you want to find him?"

"Well . . ." Kitten paused. "This is going to sound rather funny."

"Nothing connected with the Flöbbertigôbbet is remotely funny, son."

"Perhaps I should have used the word 'odd,' then. It's just, well—a friend; a new friend I made yesterday; she told me that, um; she said there's this evil thing that had come into our world—the Flöbbertigôbbet—and it's inside of me and if I wanted to fight it, I had to come here and find it."

"You came to fight evil, then. But now you want to leave?"

Kitten considered this. "I guess so; but if I do, I won't have solved the problem, and it will still be inside of me, like some awful parasite." The cat shuddered in horror.

"I don't see that you have that internal problem, son. If you were hosting the Flöbbertigôbbet inside of yourself, I could see the signs of him easily. He may have been there at one time; that's quite possible; but he isn't there now."

"My friend—she's a turtle dove; a lovely bird—she said that it, uh; he had made me into one of his soldiers, or at least was in the process of doing so."

"Did you freely agree to accept his presence in you?"

"No; I didn't even know he existed."

"Then his hold on you was probably released as you came into our world. There is a process one goes through."

"Do you mean the dying? I sort of died as I went through the Door, just for a few seconds. It was really horrible, like being nothing in a nowhere place, but it didn't last long."

"Yes, I am referring to that death, which often changes those who undergo it. They don't all change in the same way, and many who go through the dying don't appear to be altered at all, but in some cases, the presence of evil is expelled from the traveller. Have you felt different?"

"Well—I thought maybe I did react to certain things in a manner that wasn't quite normal for me, though I thought it was perhaps due to the influence of my new friend. Still; I can't exactly put my finger on it, but I appear to be a better cat than I was before. It feels like; it almost seems to be a change that goes beyond a merely intellectual alteration. I think; I think perhaps something went on that was more than just evil being expelled from me." Kitten shook his head; frustrated. "This is very difficult to describe, ma'am."

"I see."

"I wonder about something," the tabby said.

"What is that?"

"Dove—my new friend—she told me that no one who's gone through the Door I went through has ever come back. What happens to them?"

"The fates of visitors vary greatly. Some individuals are eaten by the greys, while others fail to return because they prefer to stay here for one reason or another. And of course, there are those who make the wrong choices when they are challenged by the Flöbbertigôbbet's agents, and they are absorbed into his army."

"Agents?"

"You already met two of those: the upright-walking mouse; the goldfinch."

"Oh! Those weren't just chance encounters?"

"No. The Flöbbertigôbbet would have known immediately about your entry here. It is the creature's habit to send agents who attempt to enlist or kill all newcomers."

"Neither the mouse nor the goldfinch tried to enlist or kill me."

"Yes, they did. It was the mouse's plan to entangle you in agreements of indebtedness that would cause you to become enslaved in the Flöbbertigôbbet's service. The rodent knew of your presence all along, and was merely pretending to be surprised when you tapped him on the head. When his clumsy attempt to gain your cooperation failed, the goldfinch tried to end your life by sending you into battle against a superior animal: an innocent mongoose who was nearby in the forest. You wouldn't have stood a chance against such an opponent, as you knew. It's fortunate that you were able to resist her attempt at emotional seduction; if you hadn't, she would have led you into a fight to the death against a creature who would have had no choice but to defend himself. It's typical for that lost little bird to use imaginary children as a way to destroy others." Wolf shook her head in dismay. "Now, the grey monsters: I don't like to pay them the questionable compliment of classifying such dumb beasts as agents of the Flöbbertigôbbet, though they are his. They aren't as orderly as the others: they're quite stupid, and run about killing whatever they come across; sparing only those who belong to their side; to the enemy." The canid lowered her nose in a modest bow of the head. "I am General of the army which opposes the Flöbbertigôbbet and his forces."

"Oh, my! You're a general!" Kitten knew a thing or two about such creatures. He had encountered several high-ranking military officers in his Lady's house. Being the widow of a member of ancient aristocracy, the woman felt obligated to entertain important people now and then. Her cat, however, had never been terribly interested in the stern gentlemen who came to dinner wearing fancy uniforms decorated with badges of gleaming metal and colorful ribbons. He had been dimly aware that they were warriors who claimed to fight for noble causes but, being far distanced from most of the wars and struggles of mankind, the Shorthair was only interested in whether or not these personages were willing to scratch him behind the ears, which they usually were not; being more fond of dogs than felines. This heroic general-wolf, though—Kitten had encountered her enemies in frightful close-up. He had seen her fight, and knew whom she chose to fight, and was impressed. He instinctively rose and stood at attention. "Ma'am!"

Wolf laughed, or at least did the *Canis lupus* version of such an expression of mirth. "Does this mean you want to be one of my soldiers now?"

Kitten sat down quickly. "Oh—I didn't mean that!"

"Perhaps you will consider it, and not run back home so quickly?"

"Perhaps." Kitten looked down at the floor of the den, somewhat intimidated by the wolf's importance. "Ma'am?"

"Yes?"

"I'm very thirsty."

"Of course. And you must be quite hungry as well. Would you like to go out for some breakfast?"

"Yes, please; if you can show me how to find food."

"That won't be a problem." Wolf rose and went to the den's entrance, where she addressed the trio of coyotes. "If you gentlemen would like to go about your own business, you're dismissed."

"Thank you, ma'am." First Coyote and his brothers loped away together, quickly vanishing in the thick cover of the forest.

Wolf and the tabby stepped out of the den and into the dappled sunlight, where the feline paused for a morning stretch. "Did you leave me the fish yesterday?" Kitten asked, leaning down on his forepaws as he pulled his hindquarters back.

"Yes, I left the trout. I knew you'd be hungry, and I didn't have any provisions close by, so I found an elderly fish who was willing to move on." Wolf flopped down to roll and wriggle about in the dead leaves that covered the ground, loosening up her spine.

70

"This is a most curious place," the little tiger said, sitting down to watch the wolf twisting happily about on her back.

"Your world is curious as well." Finished with her brief session of self-chiropractic, the General rolled onto her stomach and looked at the cat. "I must say, I tend to think my home is better than yours, judging from what I've heard. Your earth is quite brutal."

"Well, it has its good points. We don't have slimy grey monsters, and mice don't drive fancy sports utility vehicles and look down their noses at folks who lack a big stock portfolio. Granted, we do have a great many humans who do that—I see them at my Lady's house fairly often. But such behavior is strictly limited to people. We animals are free from shallow materialism."

"I've heard about the struggle for survival which most in your world go through in one way or another. I expect that your Lady's 'materialism' is the force which keeps you well fed, is it not? I see that you aren't a terribly thin cat."

Kitten blinked. "I'm not fat!"

"But you are most certainly not thin. What do you usually eat—where does your food come from?"

"My Lady has fresh fish brought in by helicopter from a place of clear waters that are guaranteed to be free of mercury and other pollutants. I get a bit of cheese every day—Stilton is my favorite. It's a blue-veined, creamy *fromage* made from an old English recipe. We get ours from a Nottingham dairy owned by a friend of my Lady. I get vitamin supplements as well, mixed with a crunchy cat food that keeps my teeth clean and provides a balanced diet along with the other items."

"Are these foodstuffs given to your Lady by the people who produce them?"

"No—she spends a lot of money for my food. There's a great deal of work involved in the making of fine cheese, and the fish delivery; well, helicopters are costly to maintain, and there's the cost of the petrol for them, and the trained pilot, and of course, the fishermen must be compensated for their labors, and the factories which produce my vitamins and crunchy feed: all must be paid for. My Lady has a great fortune —there's no reason why she shouldn't pay."

"You survive on your owner's wealth, yet accuse the mouse of 'shallow materialism' because he is proud of what he has acquired?"

"I am not proud of what my Lady gives me. I'm very happy to have it," Kitten paused, realizing that he didn't fully appreciate this fine diet when he had immediate access to it. Feeling a bit guilty, he continued. "I'm grateful for such wonderful food, but I don't believe that my Lady's wealth, which is in a way my wealth too, makes me better than those who don't have such comforts. I wish everyone could have what I have. Unlike the mouse, I would not accuse someone of being no one because they don't have certain luxuries. I would be inclined to share with those who lack such things, not insult them."

"As I suspected," Wolf said, "you are a good cat. That sad little materialistic mouse was once a good fellow; he was at one time a credit to his species. It's unfortunate that certain situations caused him to give in to his weaknesses instead of building his strengths. Yes, he was once a very good mouse, and I pity him for the fact that he has fallen so low as to be no more than a puppet for the Flöbbertigôbbet."

Kitten looked at the wolf; his eyes bright with fresh determination. "Perhaps you can answer the question to which the ants weren't willing to respond. Do you know where I can find the Flöbbertigôbbet?"

"He lives at the border."

"Which border?"

"The one that divides the halves. Our world is not set up like yours. There's a line—the border—that divides the sphere of our planet exactly in half. On one half live the people, with their buildings and machines, their technology and whatnot. On the other half are the free animals. There is only nature in our hemisphere; neither humans nor things of the humans are allowed here. They can't even fly their planes and helicopters over our area, though they do have satellites far out in space which look down on us. The satellites don't trouble us, however, so we just ignore their presence."

"How was all that separation managed? My world would never be able to work out a neat arrangement like that."

"In your world, animals are dominated by human technology: the bulldozers and explosives that destroy their habitats; the guns, traps, and poisons used to kill or capture them. Your world's animals are powerless to resist the weapons used against them so that people can take over their territory or make them into meals and clothing. Here in my home, things are quite different. For example, when we speak to humans, they can understand our words. But the most important difference between my world and yours is that in mine, we animals have our own power; our own weapons, so to speak—we can control the weather and tectonic plates."

"What?" Kitten was astonished. "I don't believe it!"

"Believe it, son. If the humans were to violate our pact with them, we would send natural disasters onto their hemisphere; disasters of a very serious type: super-typhoons with winds of two hundred miles an hour; hurricanes bearing relentless heavy rains that would flood cities and towns with immeasurable fathoms of water; earthquakes that could topple the best engineered of buildings; lightning storms that would devastate electrical power plants; tornadoes of such size and strength that even the deepest storm cellars would be dug up by the mighty spinning and tossed high into the air. Yes, we have power, son. We didn't want to use it against the humans at first, and resisted doing so for a very long time, but hard experience finally convinced us that we had to use it if we wanted to keep the rest of our various species alive and breathing, instead of watching them fade into a presence that exists only in libraries within the category of 'extinct animals.'"

"Well!"

"Despite all that power, our present happy status is threatened, I'm afraid. There are many humans who'd like to move into our side, and they push at their government to develop bombs that would kill all the animals in our hemisphere so quickly that we'd have no time to retaliate. Fortunately, those aggressive types are opposed by a large number of people who respect us not just for our power but for the fact that we deserve the right to live our lives in the natural environment which suits us best. They fight for us in the political houses, and have done a good job of inhibiting bomb research. Those people are our friends, and provide the carnivore and scavenger species with plant-based protein feed so we don't have to kill to eat. They leave bags of pellets at the border, and our network of providers disperses the food throughout the hemisphere, carrying the bags on their backs. The camels and elephants—they work hard to keep their brothers in nature fed." Wolf lifted a hind foot and scratched herself behind one ear. "It is for the sake of the good people that we haven't wiped out the inhabitants of the unnatural hemisphere in preventive self-defense. Some animals say that we should drown all the humans with rain storms before they develop bombs that could wipe us out; they say we should make humanity an extinct species to pay them back for what they did to so many of our kind; but I don't think it would be right. The majority of the natural population agree with me on that. That kind of mass killing would be savage, and besides, we do depend on the humans for the food that has allowed us to become truly peaceful beings."

Kitten thought of a tiny exhaust-emitting sports utility vehicle. "You say things of the humans aren't allowed here. But the mouse—his cellphone, stocks, and SUV. Aren't those things of humanity?"

"Yes and no. In the mouse's case, while those things originated in the human hemisphere, they came here by way of the Flöbbertigôbbet. His interference with the lives of natural creatures is the reason why I formed an army to fight him. He sits there on the border, hidden inside his fortress, sending grief all over the world. He's the enemy of both hemispheres. He provides animals with gadgets that suck them into a morass of inescapable debt or has us murdered by his collection of monsters. And what he does to the humans; oh, my—the things he does to those people! I wouldn't want to live their lives; that's for certain."

"Can't you send weather onto him: wipe him out with a lightning storm or something?"

"I'm afraid that wouldn't work, even if we were able to aim weather so specifically that it would destroy only a single building instead of an entire region. Sadly, we aren't able to do that with a solid measure of reliability. But even if we could, it wouldn't work against the Flöbbertigôbbet himself; only his armies. The enemy has a power of his own. He's different. He's immortal."

"Immortal, eh? And how does one fight something that's immortal?"

Wolf hung her head. "We do the best we can." The canid closed her eyes for a moment, mulling over an inner pain. Raising her head, she looked very carefully at the little tabby. "The Flöbbertigôbbet has been here as far back as anyone can remember. Sometimes I'm tempted to think that he might be a necessary and integral part of this place. And, after so many years of fighting, I'm beginning to fear that I've taken on an impossible task, trying to beat an immortal."

"I'm sure he wants you to think that, and is very glad that you do!" Kitten snorted. "Immortal, indeed! Nothing lasts forever. Everything has a beginning and an end. My universe had a beginning and will some day have an end, and so must this allegedly immortal being."

"What if we need him? Maybe evil; maybe we need grief. Perhaps without it our lives would be too easy, and we wouldn't make progress or develop character."

"Are you insane?" Kitten was furious. "That is complete and utter bull!"

"Bull? My statement is a male bovine? Who is the insane one here?"

"No, no, no—I didn't mean to say that. 'Bull' is American slang for untruth."

"Why do you use American slang? Aren't you an English cat?"

"Well, I'm an English cat now, but I was born in America and lived there when I was very, very young. That's likely where I picked up 'bull'."

"I see."

"I shall get back to my point about your untruth," Kitten said. "What I meant was; just plain natural life itself without evil is hard enough. The basic struggle for survival: it's quite difficult for most. Why would anyone need an unnatural evil that causes extraordinary and excessive sufferings when we already have natural problems like cancer or other illnesses?"

"Yes," the General responded, "I believe you have made a good point. The grief sent by the Flöbbertigôbbet is excessive and unproductive; especially the things he inspires in the humans. They kill one another for reasons that have nothing to do with survival; people become addicted to drugs and die from overdoses, leaving behind nothing but pain: why would anyone need that kind of suffering?"

The tabby snorted angrily. "Anyone who says evil is necessary is dead wrong, ma'am. I only had to see a few seconds of one small war to know that." Kitten's long white whiskers bristled. "That idea is as wrong as your belief that the Flöbbertigôbbet is so thoroughly immortal that he can't be disposed of. Somewhere, somehow, this creature had a beginning. What had a beginning can have an end. It is our job to provide that end!"

Wolf's eyes gleamed in the quiet way that suggested a smile. "Then you will fight with us?"

"Yes, ma'am. Evil stinks."

"Well and succinctly put, son. Now, let's go get breakfast."

CHAPTER FOUR

First Horse and the Grizzly

The morning meal was not as exciting to the taste buds as the fine European foodstuffs to which Kitten was accustomed, but the pellets provided by the good-hearted humans were nutritious and satisfying. After filling their stomachs with the contents of an open burlap bag that had been left nearby under a tree, the wolf and cat drank from a clear stream which ran not far from the den.

The pair started off through the forest together. "Where are we headed?" Kitten asked. "Are we going to fight the Flöbbertigôbbet now?"

"His fortress is quite far off, son. I shouldn't go on such a long trip without making certain arrangements first. For now, we'll just patrol and see how things are going today."

"Okay." The tabby began to run, stretching his short legs forward as far as he could in an attempt to keep up with the efficient trot of the big wolf. It was hard work for the house cat; not only racing to follow a much larger animal, but doing so over rough terrain to which he was not accustomed. In no time at all, the tiny tiger was loudly huffing and puffing with the effort.

Wolf looked down at the feline. "You're out of shape, I'm afraid."

"I exercise a lot in my Lady's house," the tabby protested. "I do hundreds of steps on the stairs at a dead run every morning and night. It's just that your legs are so much longer than mine." Kitten stopped and dropped his head, overcome by heavy panting.

"I'll get us a ride, son. If I call First Horse, she can carry not only you, but me as well, should I become overtired. The filly is young, while I am not. Her stamina is much greater than mine." The General was trying to be tactful, including herself in the passenger situation when it was a fact that her state of physical fitness was nothing less than astonishing.

The canid sat down and focused straight ahead, looking at nothing as she concentrated on something within. There came a soft grunt from her throat, then she turned and looked at Kitten. "First Horse will be here soon. That girl can run like you wouldn't believe! At a dark time in the distant past, a talented lady like her would have been forced to gallop in pointless circles on the humans' racetracks. Thankfully, those days vanished into history long ago."

"How . . . how did you do that?"

"Do what?"

"Call the horse. I didn't hear anything."

"Oh—that's right. You other-worlders can't do that to the extent to which we can. I forget sometimes."

"We can't do what?"

"Our powers of communication are a bit more advanced than yours. We can hear or call out to any other members of nature at any time using our minds. It's quite a bit harder than using voices and ears, and we can't transmit complex information as well as we can with words, but a simple message can usually get through, and it goes much farther than it would in the ordinary physical way. I believe some of you other-world animals can do similar things. I have heard that in your home, there is an inner method of communication that joins far-flung birds together in one physical place at a precise moment so they can flock *en masse* on their migratory journey."

"Is that anything like the way that cattle move to higher ground days before a flood comes?"

"No. Prophetic powers are not the same as silent communication."

"Hm. Maybe it's like when my Lady's been gone from the house, and she's coming back home in her car —I know she's on her way before I actually hear the automobile."

"That's right. I use the same type of mental faculty to call my troops, and it's how I found the old trout who agreed to be your supper." Wolf paused, hearing a distant thunder that was rapidly growing louder. A crashing could be heard coming through the underbrush—something large and heavy was plowing down chunks of the forest as it made its way forward in a pounding, booming path of destruction.

The canid's tail thumped the ground. "First Horse couldn't sneak up on a foe if her very life depended on a silent approach. Oh, well—she does leave cleared and convenient paths in her wake!"

A nearby birch sapling went down as over the snapping trunk shot an exploding presence of unadulterated power: the General's First Horse. She was a beautiful thing; clad in a shining pale hair coat the color of moonlight and crowned by a rich mane of silver shot through with ivory and deepest charcoal grey. Her great eyes were black but gentle, showing a nature that was innocent yet bold.

The equine skidded into a sliding stop before her commanding officer. Kitten could see that her fine hide was flecked with soft bits of red; tiny spots of pigment which brought to mind his Lady's slender Arabian stallion. The flecks of rusty scarlet on that Arab's coat were referred to as the Blood of Allah, and thought to be marks of great distinction. This red-flecked lady, clearly a hot-blood of some sort, was not only pretty but built for hard work; with a bulging, muscled chest and solid hindquarters carried on well-boned, sturdy legs. Ineradicable signs of her occupation were borne here and there on her head and body: traces of war wounds that would never go away; for instance, the ragged edge of her right ear, where she had been bitten by a grey monster in her youth. First Horse was, after all, a war-horse, and could not be expected to mirror the flawless, shiny show-beasts that populated Kitten's civilized country hamlet. First Horse would not for a moment have felt inferior to such pretty, pampered equine pets; wearing her scarry badges of victory in battle with a warrior's pride.

Kitten looked up at the soldier and sighed. He had carried a secret admiration for horses since he first came to his Lady's home. Denied the opportunity to visit the stables and see them up close, he would spend happy mornings at a high attic window; watching as the graceful, strong creatures were exercised on the grounds of the estate. The feline had often wished that he could leap onto one of their backs and go for a ride himself; to feel the wind whistling past his ears as a first-rate Thoroughbred stretched out its long legs and went into a flat-out racing gallop. Proper English house cats, however, were not encouraged to do such things.

First Horse, snorting and puffing with healthy vigor, began to prance in place before her general and the tabby. Sinewy legs of solid muscle kicked high to break sharply at the knee and then dropped, like slow springs, only to bounce back into the break again after the first contact with the ground; as though the equine's alabaster hooves feared the gentle kiss of the earth, yet couldn't resist seeking it, over and over again. Erupting out of the brief controlled prance and into wild self-expression, the filly turned and kicked up her back feet in celebration of a giddy feel-good happiness. One big jump-kick, two big jump-kicks, one near-somersault, and she dashed forward into an abrupt gallop that halted as soon as it had begun; chunks of disturbed earth flying into the air as hooves dug into *terra firma* for a flashy halt. In a final explosion of showing off, the quadruped kicked her hind feet up so high that Kitten feared the equine might tumble forward into a spine-shattering roll. First Horse was not so foolish as to perform such a self-destructive feat, however, and brought her heels back down to earth a split millisecond before her equilibrium reached the endangered point. Standing suddenly quiet, she bowed her head to her superior.

Wolf's tail drummed against the ground in a hearty expression of appreciation for the athletic show. "What's got into my girl today?" she asked. "Did you find a field of oats someplace and stuff yourself into this veritable tizzy of excess energy?"

First Horse let out an eardrum-shattering whinny of *joie de vivre*. "How did you know?"

"Just a lucky guess, young lady."

The equine snorted happily. "Golden oats they were, ma'am; rich and golden and sweet."

"You didn't overdo it, did you? You know how sensitive your stomach is."

"I was careful." First Horse's nose bobbed up and down as she strove to avoid the attentions of an overly friendly fly. "Why did you call me, ma'am?"

"Kitten here—may I call you Kitten, son?"

"That is how I am known, ma'am," the tabby replied.

"Kitten needs a ride. He's new to the forest—new to our world, in fact—and quite worn out."

"I would be happy to help. Have you ridden a horse before?" the filly asked.

"No." Kitten's eyes were huge with excitement. "Never even been near a horse!" he declared.

"I see. Well, riding shouldn't be too hard for an agile feline. Just keep yourself balanced: sit up straight." First Horse eyed Kitten's rigid, curled-up tail and distorted spine, which would force the cat to sit at a lopsided and therefore dangerously unbalanced angle. "No; don't sit at all. Stretch out on your stomach and hang onto my mane with both paws. You'll be fine. We don't need to run, do we?" she asked the General.

"I don't expect to move at high speed. We're just on patrol."

"All right." First Horse lowered her forequarters to the ground, putting herself into a deep bow. "Hop on, little fellow."

"Uh . . ." Kitten was trembling with a combination of terror and joy. "Should I retract my claws as I jump? I might slip off if I keep them in."

"I can take a few punctures, friend. Do whatever is best for you."

"Okay!" Kitten leapt up onto the back of the big quadruped. Arranging himself along her spine, he grabbed onto her silver mane with his claws. "I think I'm stabbing you. Am I hurting you?"

"It's all right—you just have a grip on my mane, not my hide. Now, hold on—I'm getting up." First Horse straightened her forelegs and stood erect as Kitten held on for dear life. "Calm down, little fellow; there's nothing to be afraid of."

"I'm not afraid!" the tabby protested.

"Yes, you are. I can smell your fear. You're scared to death."

"Well; okay, I am. What if I fall?"

"You're a cat! Are you trying to tell me you've never left the ground before?"

Kitten recalled his mountaineering expeditions through the Lady's house: his climbs to the tops of pieces of tall furniture from which he had ascended to high shelves where he could sit and look down upon the heads of the household staff as they went about their business, and how as a very small and somewhat clumsy kitten he would fall, roll in the air like a tumbling acrobat, and suffer no ill effects whatsoever as he landed on the floor. "I'm being irrational," he muttered.

"Yes, you are. The only way you could get hurt would be if you fell off and I stepped on you, and that's not going to happen. I'll feel it immediately if you fall, and I'll look out for you. Unlike cats, I can see all around myself; not just in front. That is the advantage of having eyes on the sides of one's head. Now, relax!"

"Okay."

"Where are we off to, ma'am?" First Horse inquired.

"The third sector—there's been an especially large increase in enemy activity there. Huge numbers of greys and agents have been on the prowl, and a valued chimpanzee was recruited into the hostile camp. Seems she was conquered by the offer of cosmetic surgery: always wanted to have a perky custom-made nose like a human debutante, apparently."

"You're joking!"

"I'm not. It was the youngest female who worked with the third sector elephants, loading feedbags onto their backs. Did you know her?"

"I thought I knew her, but if she caved in for the sake of a clearly insane vanity, I obviously didn't know that chimp at all."

"We're getting to be as emotionally vulnerable as the humans, I'm afraid. That's where evolutionary progress gets us, eh?"

First Horse shook her head. "I guess . . ." The equine snorted wetly in disgust. "A chimp with a human nose—that's something I hope I never have to see."

Kitten listened to the exchange, overcome by wonder. "What a strange place this is," he whispered to himself.

The tiny tiger clung to the horse's mane as the trio started off through the forest. As they progressed, the trees began to thin out, and they soon came to an area of open grassland. "Down this slope," Wolf said as she turned to her right. "A good stream is down there, and we don't want to get too far away from water."

"Yes, ma'am." First Horse followed her superior officer.

The General stopped suddenly. "Wait—someone's in trouble!"

The equine halted. Her ears went forward, and a second later Kitten heard a deep-voiced roar coming from a rock-bordered gully on their left. "Oh, no," the cat muttered.

"Hang on!" First Horse shouted. Kitten went into a crouch and, clenching his body like a fist, dug his claws deep into horsehide; holding a secure position as the filly exploded into a gallop.

One would think that a fit young horse could outrun an old wolf, but this was not the case. Showing one of the many reasons for her success as a general, the canid proceeded to outpace the equine at an amazing rate of speed; shooting ahead like a rocket that streaked toward its goal with no regard for the normal rules of physics. Her legs had become a flashing blur that was barely visible as she flew ahead of the pale quadruped, and in a fleeting moment, she had left the filly far behind. "Come on!" the General yelled, disappearing into the gully.

First Horse pushed on and a few seconds later entered the ravine; the tabby's hind end swaying dangerously as the equine made a sharp turn round a big rock. Seeing what was in the center of the small canyon, she slammed to an abrupt halt that sent Kitten flying to the ground. Landing with his usual adroitness, he rolled once and jumped to his feet.

It was an ugly, ugly scene indeed. Three grey monsters were dancing with hideous glee about a lone grizzly bear. He was a truly noble beast: a splendid example of the great *Ursus horribilis* who in Kitten's world inhabits certain sections of remote wilderness in North America. Tied upright to a towering sequoia tree, the gigantic bear stood over ten feet tall. The mighty creature's lower left extremity was caught in a giant steel-jawed trap; its vicious metal teeth causing copious amounts of blood to flow from its victim's leg. The grizzly's arms, stretched back around the trunk of the column-like tree, were tied behind him with heavy strips of thick leather. His face was striped with scarlet where the greys had cut him with metal hooks attached to long poles.

The General was trotting in a circle around the dancing trio of torturers. Having warned them to leave the bear alone and finding that her words were being ignored, Wolf was now deciding which monster she should attack first. After brief deliberation, she chose the middle-sized grey; a beast about three times her size: a formidable foe, but one the canid's strength gave her the ability to overcome. In Kitten's home, a wolf's jaws can put out a crushing pressure of fifteen hundred pounds per square inch, and in this world, wolves were larger and more powerful than that. Shouting at First Horse, "Take the big one!" the General leapt forward, mouth wide-open and deadly teeth fully exposed, and fastened her set of four two-inch-long canine fangs onto the throat of the grey.

First Horse snorted, let out an ear-piercing cry of wild rage, and ran to the biggest monster. Rearing straight up from her hind, she was almost as tall as her opponent. As the beast made an attempt to slash her exposed stomach with his sharp metal hook, she used her front hooves to kick the weapon out of his hands. The grey roared and tried to bite the war-horse's neck, but she had learned from the mistakes of her youth and dodged his teeth; responding to the monster's move with a soundly placed hoof to the head.

Kitten was blind with fury. He had seen something similar to this before, on his Lady's television set. A station doing a story on animal treatment had shown film of an ancient pastime enjoying underground popularity in Pakistan: bear-baiting; an illegal entertainment. Certain men of the nation derived pleasure from chaining small black bears to poles and watching as dogs tore them to pieces. This was a pastime whose appeal the young feline had been incapable of understanding, as it clearly lacked the nobility of a natural animal's hunt, and he had proceeded to turn his eyes away from the violent images of tortured bears and happy men. Kitten's Lady, seeing this cruelty on her television screen, had shouted several foul obscenities at the set before quickly turning it off.

The gruesome scene being played out in the gully, however, wasn't a two-dimensional television image—it couldn't be turned off. This was real, and horrible, and Kitten was so furious that he could barely see, and he certainly could not take time to think. Rushing forward, the tiny acrobat made an incredible leap up onto the head of the smallest grey as it poked with its hook at the face of the helpless, roaring bear. Holding on as best he could, the tabby began to scratch at the Thing's eyes.

The monster dropped his weapon and, grabbing with his hands, attempted to pull the cat off. The feline had no intention of being dislodged, and clung to the slimy skull with all he had. Unfortunately, there wasn't much to hang onto, just skin over spongy bone, and the grey soon succeeded in loosening the tabby from his chosen battle post. Clutching the cat in one hand, the creature popped him into its huge mouth. A second later, there was a powerful kick to the monster's midsection, and Kitten was forcibly ejected from the grotesque cavity that had held him.

Hitting the ground hard, he rolled once and stood up. First Horse was before him; the downed monster's somewhat flattened head under her right forefoot. "Thank you, Miss," Kitten said.

"You did well, little fellow. You distracted the thing so it couldn't continue to hurt the bear. It was grand of you to take on someone so much larger than yourself."

Kitten was embarrassed. "Some might say it was stupid."

"No, no—it was quite grand." The war-horse bobbed her dusky nose. "We won the battle; all three greys are dead." She removed her foot from the monster's head. "They won't torture any more animals."

The tabby looked at the grizzly, who was slumped against the tree trunk. The General had cut his leather bindings with her fangs and the bear was attempting to stay upright, nearly unconscious from pain and loss of blood. Wolf was examining the steel trap that held his leg. "First Horse!" she called. "Help me with this!"

The filly went to the General's side. Looking at the trap, she flipped her ears back in anger. "I think I can open it with the bear's help. Are you able, sir?"

The grizzly nodded weakly. "I'll try."

"You pull at that part there—the part where there aren't any metal teeth—when I tell you to, and I'll push here." First Horse placed her front hooves against a smooth inside edge of the trap's jaws. "Now, pull!" The bear tugged with both paws at his assigned section as the filly put her weight and strong muscles against hers, and the trap opened slightly; just enough for the grizzly to pull his mangled leg out. The bear released his grip on the trap as First Horse jumped out of its way; whinnying in horror at the awful noise the device made as it snapped its bone-crushing jaws shut.

Kitten eyed the vicious trap. "One of the Flöbbertigôbbet's generous donations to this hemisphere, I expect."

"Yes, son." Wolf went to the bear's head. The huge animal had collapsed onto the ground at the base of the tree, and lay quietly passive as the canid gently licked his facial wounds.

First Horse was engaged in the process of examining the grizzly's injured leg. She sniffed and peeked and thought a bit, grinding her back teeth in consternation. Finally, she spoke. "Ma'am."

"Yes?" Wolf broke off her ministrations.

"This situation is very bad. We're going to need; we're going to need a miracle if this fellow is to walk again."

"I see." The canid sighed. "A miracle it will be, then."

"Are you sure you're up to it, ma'am?"

"Thank you, First Horse—I know I'm not young anymore. But I believe I still have enough left in me that I can survive the effort. If this bear can't walk with both hind legs, he can't live, and he's young enough that he should have the chance to enjoy a good long future ahead of him. I won't sit by and let him die. Look at him—he's so beautiful."

Both Kitten and the equine had to agree with that. Even lying limp on the ground, the huge grizzly was a wonderful thing to behold. Thick, deep-brown fur covered the great beast in a shining, healthful coat; a raiment so glorious it made him seem a king. His long-clawed front paws, resting passively on the ground where they had fallen as the bear flopped onto his back, were so big that the little tabby could have curled up in an open palm and made it his bed. And those great furry back feet! They had to be the biggest feet in creation. Maybe they weren't quite as round as an elephant's foot, but they were certainly equal in length to such appendages, and far more grand with the toes' elegant curved talons. Yes, the grizzly bear was beautiful indeed.

The tabby eyed the huge pile of lustrous fur marred by bleeding wounds. "He must be in a lot of pain."

"I'm not sure if he's still conscious to any degree," the General said, "but if he is, he's suffering greatly. I've got to do something quick."

First Horse backed off from the grizzly. "Come with me, little cat." The tabby followed. A long stone's throw away from the mountain of brown fur, the equine lowered herself to the ground. "Here, Kitten. Sit up against me—things will likely get a bit rough." The feline obediently took a seat; leaning back against the quadruped's bent forelegs.

The General began to circle the bear at a trot, including the tree in her generous orbit. A soft whimpering could be heard coming from the canid; so subtle that Kitten wasn't certain it was her voice at all: perhaps it was just an undercurrent of the whispering wind that had suddenly risen out of nowhere. Odd how the breeze came up just as the wolf started to circle, and odder still how it blew roundabout in a gentle whirlwind that surrounded the bear and tree in the same path the General was pacing.

The low whimpering grew louder, and the whirlwind increased the force of its spinning. The wolf trotted faster and broke into a circular lope. Clouds of dust and loose dirt began to stir up with the wind; forming a wall about the bear that soon obscured all sight of him. Wolf ran with the whirling barrier, gradually increasing the size of her circle. The girth of the spinning dust-wall increased in accordance with the canid's paces; sending out secondary winds that blew in random gusts to fill the gully with flying debris. Closing his eyes tightly to shut out the ricocheting dirt, Kitten crawled into the sheltered space behind First Horse's forelegs to avoid the open, churning air.

Wolf let out a loud cry as she came to an abrupt halt. The whirlwind continued to spin as she stood at its perimeter; tail to the moving wall, nose pointing at the eastern sky. The canid emitted a mournful howl, and was answered by an explosion from above. Fingers of lightning reached down into the gully as claps of thunder shook the ground.

The General collapsed onto the earth and the wind slowed, then stopped entirely. As the dust and debris settled, Kitten could see the bear again; still lying on the ground but no longer bearing scarlet stripes on his face. The exposed, splintered bone and bleeding flesh of his mangled leg were no longer in evidence, either —the limb was whole again.

The grizzly sat up and looked first at the wolf, then at the horse and cat. "Help her!" he cried.

Kitten leapt out of his safe cave behind First Horse's knees, and she jumped up and ran to her superior officer. "Ma'am!"

The wolf didn't answer.

"Ma'am!" Kitten shouted as he ran after the horse. Rushing to the canid, he began to lick her nose.

The wolf twitched violently, startling the tabby. A deep inhalation, then she exhaled in a mighty sigh. "Well." The General rolled over into a sitting position. "Well."

"You did it, ma'am. The bear is healed." First Horse nickered with joy.

"We did it, you mean. The whole of nature did it."

"Of course, ma'am." The equine bobbed her nose up and down. "You scared me out of my wits—I thought the effort had killed you."

"I have to admit . . . it almost did."

The bear gathered himself onto his feet and stood upright, eliciting an involuntary scream from the cat. "You are so big!" the tabby cried.

"Yes, I am. Do you think you could leap as high as my head?" The grizzly roared with delight. "I saw how you jumped onto the grey monster's nasty cranium as you so very bravely defended me. You're more than welcome to fly up onto my head, if you like."

"I can't jump that high, sir." Kitten was awed.

"Here, then; I'll give you a lift." The bear reached down and plucked the cat from his spot on the ground, transporting the feline to the furry slope of his well-muscled right shoulder. "Hang on now, little fellow; don't go sliding off."

The tabby grabbed onto the grizzly's thick coat; overcome by excitement. "I don't believe it—I'm on Ursus horribilis's shoulder!"

"Well, now—that's a rather nasty thing to call me, son! Am I really so horrible?" The bear turned his head and looked the cat closely in the eye.

Kitten looked at his new friend's black snout; a mere inch away from the tiny tiger's delicate pink nose. "I'm sorry, sir; that's what they call your kind in my world."

"Oh—you're an other-worlder. No wonder your manners are, um; different from ours."

"How did you get into that awful trap?"

"It was hidden in the grass. When the greys set such traps, the jaws are opened and flat so the device is only slightly higher than the ground. They had concealed it in the vegetation by the base of that tree. When I went to sit in the shade . . ." The grizzly fell silent.

"That's awful! How can anyone do such an evil thing?"

"Trying to understand a senseless horror like evil—it's an impossible task, Kitten." The General, overcome by disgust, showed her front teeth for a brief moment. "The only thing we can do is fight it."

"I'll consider myself lucky," the bear said. "If I'd been a small animal, the trap might have caught me by the neck and taken off my head. This fine wolf wouldn't have been able to do anything for me then."

First Horse took note of the way in which the bear addressed the canid by a fairly ordinary label. "This fine wolf is the General."

The grizzly was startled, and slapped his forehead. "Ma'am! I'm sorry; I didn't know! I should have known, of course. I've heard so much about you. I should've recognized you."

"It's all right, Bear. You're not a member of my troops; there's no need for an apology."

"Ma'am?"

"Yes?"

"Could I join your army, please? I'm not an experienced fighter, outside of the occasional short-lived quarrels with brothers and cousins, but I do have a large and very strong body to offer up to the cause."

"We would be honored to have such a magnificent soldier amongst our ranks. Welcome!" Wolf extended a forefoot.

The bear leaned down as he set Kitten carefully on the ground, then took the canid's paw into his own and shook firmly. After releasing the wolf's foot, he straightened up again to his full standing height. "What's the first task you have for me, ma'am?"

"We must get rid of that trap, and the weapons as well—those horrible hooked things."

"That's going to take some doing. The trap is so heavy that it held me down when I was in it. I can't imagine how those greys managed to get it here to begin with."

"Probably used a bloody sports utility vehicle!" Kitten declared. "A gold one; a great big fat shiny one with an aluminum alloy V8 engine equipped with two allied signal T25 turbochargers and a maximum torque of four hundred Nm spinning at four thousand two hundred and fifty revolutions per minute and the whole package going from zero to one hundred kilometers per hour in four point nine; yes, four point nine seconds!" The little tabby had apparently spent a bit too much time on the lap of a thrill-addicted race-car-driving petrol head who made frequent yet futile attempts to romance the feline's Lady. Poor Kitten: the oddest things do tend to leap into one's mind when one is under severe and extraordinary stress.

"Turbochargers?" Wolf's eyes opened wide in surprise. "Excuse me?"

The tabby tucked his white chin under. "It's been a rough morning," he mumbled.

The General considered the little feline as the filly and bear examined him with concerned eyes. "Poor Kitten," the canid said. "It's been a very hard day for the young one."

"If he wants to explode into gibberish now and then," the grizzly said, "that's fine with me. He did his best to protect me, and I won't forget it."

Kitten hung his head. "I need a nap," he said.

"Yes, you do, son," Wolf replied. "Why don't you get some rest while we dispose of the weapons?"

"Yes, ma'am." Kitten spotted a pile of dry leaves in the shade of a tree. "I'll go over there." Trotting to the soft bed, he flopped down on his side and fell into immediate sleep.

"Now—the trap," the General said. "I believe the most practical thing to do is bury it, along with the hooked poles. We can dig a deep hole right next to the trap, throw the hooks in first, then push the trap over the edge so it falls on top of the weapons. That will make it harder for the Flöbbertigôbbet's servants to get at the hooks if they try to dig them out."

"How long do you think it'll take for the trap's workings to rust solid?" First Horse asked.

"It won't take long at all if we dump the greys' corpses on top of it. You know how corrosive their body fluids are."

"Yes, that will do the trick. But we'll need a very large hole to bury all those things. Even with the three of us, it'll take hours to dig. We need help."

"I'll find out if there's anyone suitable in the area." Wolf sat down and turned her focus inside herself. After concentrating in silence for a minute or so, she spoke. "We're in luck. There's a family of mastiffs not far off; also a group of wart hogs."

"Wonderful—all good diggers!" The filly nodded in approval.

"Let's get started." The General rose to her feet and went to the trap. Picking a spot not too close to the sequoia's main roots, she began to dig in the usual canine fashion.

First Horse joined in, striking at the hard earth with her front hooves, as Bear went to work with his clawed forepaws. Progress was slow for the first few minutes, but things went much faster after the family of ten absolutely gigantic fawn-coated, black-faced dogs arrived; accompanied by a group of eight wart hogs. In

100

a short time, the shallow hole began to turn into a full-fledged pit.

When the cavity was finished, all the animals climbed out of it. Wolf stood at the pit's edge and addressed the mastiffs and wild hogs. "Thank you for your help," she said. "It was most generous of you to respond to my summons at a moment's notice."

"Our pleasure, ma'am," the mastiff patriarch answered. "We would hate to miss an opportunity to render useless such awful implements."

"And we," declared a wart hog, "take great comfort from the burial of these horrid weapons. May I throw in the first hook?"

"Please do," Wolf replied.

The wart hog scooped up one of the hooked poles with her curved tusks and carried it, carefully balanced, to the edge of the pit. As she tossed it in, there was a great cheer. Two of the younger mastiffs picked up the remaining hooks in their mouths and dropped them into the hole, accompanied by more shouts of approval.

"Bear—would you and First Horse kindly push the trap into the pit?" Wolf requested.

"We'd be honored, ma'am." The grizzly joined the filly under the tree. Showing the great strength hidden within her gracefully arched neck, First Horse put her nose to the heavy trap and, aided by the powerful arms of the bear, pushed it over onto its side and then into the pit. As it fell, the weight of the device snapped two of the hooked poles in half; eliciting cheers from the crowd.

"Now—who wants to help me throw in the greys?"

This question was greeted with silence.

"I don't blame you for your reluctance," Wolf said. "I know they're disgusting and utterly foul, but we have to get them in there if we wish to do this right."

There were a good many averted eyes in the crowd.

"Come on, now! There's a stream nearby where all can wash themselves afterward! It's not such a big thing, is it?"

"I have to use my mouth to move things about," a mastiff stated. "Do you expect me to put my jaws around one of those evil-smelling monsters so I can drag it to the hole?"

"I'll do it," the grizzly sighed. "I'm the only one of the lot who has arms. Stay where you are, please, ma'am." He grabbed hold of the gruesome bodies one by one, dragged them to the pit's edge, and tossed the slimy forms atop the trap. As he dumped in the last one, there was a loud cheer. "Thank you, thank you." *Ursus horribilis* bowed graciously, his beautiful fur coat covered with grey-green mucus. "Now, where is that stream?" Wolf pointed to her left, and the bear dropped onto all fours and ran from the gully; muttering to himself about unnatural mucusoids.

"Thank you again!" the General cried to the crowd. "I shall remember you all."

"And we shall remember you, ma'am," a big wart hog declared. "You're the leader who put an end to a terrible horror."

"At least for the moment I did," Wolf said softly. Raising her voice, she asked, "Now—can you do the final burying for me?"

"With pleasure!" a mastiff replied.

"Then we shall be on our way." The dogs and wart hogs began to transfer the mounds of freshly dug earth back into the pit, and Wolf went to the sleeping Kitten, who had not opened one eye throughout the entire operation. She nudged him gently with her nose. "Wake up!"

The feline blinked wearily. "Where's my cheese?"

"Cheese? Kitten—you're not in England anymore, remember?"

"Right." The tabby sat up. "What's going on?"

"We buried the weapons," Wolf replied, "and Bear is off taking a bath. I believe you could use one, too. You didn't come out of the grey's mouth entirely clean, you know."

Kitten looked at his paws, matted with dried slime. "Gross! I can't lick that off."

"Come—let's go to the stream. Do you want to walk, or ride the filly? It's a short distance. You can ride on me, if you want to."

"I'd like that!" The tiny tiger jumped up onto the wolf's shoulders and grabbed the thick fur of her neck.

"I'll run ahead and join the grizzly, ma'am, if you don't mind," First Horse said. "I'm very much in need of a drink."

"Go ahead." Wolf nodded in assent, and the filly took off at a gallop.

The General did her best to stay at a walk that would be comfortable for the passenger on her back. It wasn't a natural pace for her, being a creature who seemed to be always on the run, but she could manage to slow down and take it easy when the need arose. As she walked, she thought of the way the valiant feline had leapt onto the head of the grey. "I must say, Kitten; your behavior back there during the battle was most impressive."

"It was?"

"Yes—you were very brave; downright heroic. However, I recall you telling a certain finch that you would not kill for her or anyone else. It seems to me that you would've killed the grey if you had been physically able to do so."

"I think I would have, ma'am, and I'm sorry to say that I likely wouldn't have regretted such an act. Why is that? Why does it seem right? I was so certain that killing was always wrong."

"Killing is never good. Unfortunately, it was the only option we had aside from sitting by and watching as the monsters tortured the grizzly. I know what those greys are like, and simply wounding them wouldn't have worked. Once their group blood-lust gets up, the only way to stop them is to kill them. They change when there's more than one of them; they become more dangerous." Wolf snorted softly. "I suppose if we were humans, and had opposing thumbs and various devices at our disposal, we could have captured the greys and imprisoned them instead of killing them. But that is not our way."

"I believe the killing of the monsters was a necessary evil; one of those awful things usually called a 'compromise.'" Kitten frowned; his ears flattening against his head. "I don't like that word."

"It's a hard thing to swallow at times. When I was young, I thought I'd be able to get through life without ever making a single compromise. I would always be perfect, noble, and do the right thing, no matter what. But the Flöbbertigôbbet started flinging his various antagonisms into my sphere of existence, and proceeded to constantly put me between a rock and a hard place where no matter how carefully I chose, I ended up with something no better than the least awful choice of the available evils. No; constant nobility and absolute perfection: those things might be attainable in the afterlife, but not this place, nor in your world, either. I don't like killing the enemy, but since my only option is to sit by and let them carry out horrible atrocities, I have little choice." Wolf shook her head. "In my world, the idealistic perfection of nonviolent resistance is not an acceptable choice. If I sat by and did nothing as the grizzly was tortured, the god of the wolves would no longer love me, and I would no longer love myself."

The stream came into view as the two travelers emerged from a grouping of large boulders. Bear, wet but clean, was lounging on the brook's grassy bank; chewing with gusto on a cluster of juicy purple berries he had found. First Horse was standing in the bubbling creek; watching happily as refreshing currents swirled about her feet.

Kitten looked at the pristine grassland spread out about them in unspoiled perfection; its waves of luscious greenery rippling in the soft breeze. Overhead, the sky was a clear blue untouched by even a hint of chemical brown. Around the cat were creatures both predatory and vegetarian; animals living in peace with one another. If not for the lurking presence of the Flöbbertigôbbet and his subjects, this hemisphere would have been a paradise. "This is a wonderful place," the feline said. "I can see why you fight so hard to protect it."

"We are very lucky to have such a home," the General replied.

"I've been wondering about something," the tabby ventured.

"Yes, son?"

"If you and the other hunter species don't prey on your fellow animals anymore; well—in my world, predators were once a natural means of population control, and now in many areas the utter extinction or low population of large predators has led to overpopulation of other species. For example, in the United States, housing suburbs are being encroached upon by coyotes. They no longer have to compete with wolves, so they're breeding in great numbers. They kill people's pet cats." Kitten sighed deeply, then continued. "In many regions of America, deer are no longer killed by wolves or mountain lions and have to be hunted by people because there are so many that there isn't enough wild foliage for them to eat. The humans hunt them, so they say, to prevent the animals from starving to death. Guess a bullet is better than prolonged hunger."

"Your world's ecosystem is out of balance, son."

"That's not my point. My point is—if you're not killing each other, how is the population kept down? There doesn't seem to be any overcrowding here. How long has it been since there were predator-prey relationships in this world?"

"A good many centuries."

"Really? So why aren't there huge flocks of deer gobbling up all this lovely green grass? Is the Flöbbertigôbbet killing off so many animals that he's become the means of population control?"

"No." Wolf stopped at the edge of the stream, and Kitten climbed down from her back. "We have our own population control. First Horse!"

"Yes, ma'am?" The equine reluctantly lifted her eyes from the glittering, bubbling waters which had been keeping her entertained with their beauty.

"You go into regular fertile seasons every year, correct?"

"Yes, ma'am."

"Have you gotten pregnant yet?"

"No, ma'am. We have enough horses—there is no need for more at the moment."

"Don't you long for children?" Kitten asked.

"Of course I do! But I must look at the big picture. If I had a child when one wasn't needed, and everyone else saw me doing that and decided it was a great idea and did the same, there would soon be a shortage of grass and severe overcrowding. The children would go hungry and be deprived of the wide open spaces they need to run free and exercise. It would be irresponsible and selfish for me to breed when there are already plenty of horses."

"I've seen no horses other than you."

"You've just barely arrived, little cat. Trust me—there are a great many equines here."

"First Horse," the General said.

"Yes, ma'am."

"Before we go into the next sector, we should enlarge our numbers. Why don't you summon your troops? You can prove your breed's abundance to Kitten and strengthen our patrol party as well. I'm getting a feeling—a quite strong feeling—that the situation is going to be very bad in that parcel of land. We're going to need a lot of help."

"Yes, ma'am." First Horse left the stream. Standing on the bank next to the lounging bear, she lowered her head. Closing her eyes, she snorted softly three times. Opening her eyes again, she raised her nose to the sky and released a high-pitched whinny that was only slightly less loud than an exploding crack of thunder.

Kitten winced as the deafening neigh of the horse assaulted the thin skin of his sensitive eardrums. "She doesn't call as quietly as you do, ma'am," he whispered to the wolf.

"No—First Horse can be quite exuberant in her communication style."

A moment later, what seemed to be rolling thunder could be heard coming from a distance. Kitten wondered why there was no explosion of lightning to go with this deep reverberating boom, but quickly realized that the rumbling came from the earth, not the heavens. The feline looked to his right—from the top of a high grassy knoll came a racing quartet of mountain ponies, followed by a huge herd made up of every conceivable type of horse.

Solid footfalls punched the earth as the group of beefy chestnut-colored ponies fought to stay in the lead of the surging equine ocean; their sturdy legs pumping high with aggressive energy as they raced forward. They were marvelous: four effervescent miniature draft horses who pounded the ground at a mad deadline run; ivory feathers on kicking fetlocks streaming behind them, ripply cream-colored manes of gloriously hairy excess flowing from the bulging musculature of strong necks. Their eyes were bright and intelligent; their pace happy and enthusiastic. These ponies were abundant in life, and though heavy-horse ancestry seemed to be implied in their stocky builds, no heaviness was reflected in the flying movement that sped them toward their goal.

Close at their heels, a churning wave of equine flesh rose up and poured over the hillock. Jet black, snow white, deep brown, gleaming red, dappled grey, soft beige, warm chestnut: every conceivable color was seen in the coats of the vast army that thundered forward in a flood of solid-muscled power. Small round horses, tall narrow horses, medium sensible horses, giant show-off horses: all were there in the great herd.

Kitten, overcome by the sight, began to scream in loud meows. This was truly the most exciting thing he had ever seen. Jumping onto a large boulder where he could have a better view, he watched as the herd crossed the stream at speed; some horses leaping over the brook, others splashing through the waters.

The tight-knit group loosened up as it slowed down, breaking its solid flowing mass into individual bodies as the horses stopped to drink or laugh gaily; intoxicated by the fun all had just enjoyed. One of the mountain ponies trotted up to Kitten's boulder and addressed the cat. "Hey! I heard about you! New chap, eh?"

The tabby bobbed his head up and down. "You're a Haflinger! My Lady has a pony just like you—he pulls a cart for her."

"Really? I'd have a proper name, then, if I lived in your world? And a job as well? Goodness gracious!" The bold little pony tossed his head with vigor, sending his wavy platinum-blonde mane flying in every direction.

"Kitten!" Wolf called out. "You need to take your bath now! Kindly get in the water and clean yourself while I confer with the equines."

"Yes, ma'am." The cat jumped down from his rock and went to the stream, accompanied by the mountain pony.

"Watch out for the horses' feet!" Wolf cried.

"Yes, ma'am!" the feline answered. He looked around for a spot in the brook that was relatively free of prancing hooves.

"How'd you get that awful stuff on yourself?" the pony inquired.

"A grey put me in its mouth." Kitten took a deep breath as he pondered the idea of voluntarily getting himself wet all over. It was a horrible thought, but there seemed to be no choice. He entered the waters. "It spit me out when First Horse kicked it."

"Yikes! That had to be darned unpleasant." The Haflinger's eyes showed heartfelt sympathy. "There's some dried slime on your back—you'll need to get down and roll."

"Thanks." The cat dropped down and did a quick turnover in the shallow water. "You horses were, uh; summoned to go along with the General on her patrol of the third sector." The tabby left the stream. Shaking himself, he fluffed out his wet fur and stood in the warm sun to dry. "There's supposed to be; what did I hear someone say? Oh, yes—there's increased enemy activity, especially in that sector. Is it far off?"

"Not terribly; a couple of hours or so at a fast trot. If we leave now, we'll reach it well before nightfall." The pony looked carefully at the tiny tiger. "I heard a rumor that the, uh; increased activity—it has something to do with you."

"Me? How on earth . . ." Kitten remembered that he was no longer on the earth he was accustomed to. "How could I cause increased enemy activity?"

"I don't know. I just know what I heard."

"Oh. Well—when we go, may I ride on you? Your spine is quite a bit closer to the ground than First Horse's."

"Tend to fall off, do you?"

"I'm new at this riding business. The falling doesn't hurt all that much, but it does upset me."

"I understand. You're more than welcome to come along on me."

"Thanks."

The pony looked over at the wolf, who was conversing with an exceedingly tall black horse. "We'll be leaving shortly—the General isn't one to waste time when there's trouble. Go ahead and hop on." The Haflinger bent his forelegs and lowered himself to the ground, and Kitten clambered onto his back; slipping and sliding as he tried to climb up without hurting the equine. "I have a tough hide," the blonde said. "You needn't worry about hurting me. Go ahead and use your claws."

"Thank you very much, sir—I shall." The tabby positioned himself atop the pony's withers and clutched a pawful of mane.

"A word of advice: you'll stay on better if you practice a good balanced position instead of trying to rely on your ability to hang on with your claws. Center yourself along my spine and concentrate on keeping your weight in a place where, if I should suddenly

111

come to a stop, you'll stay on instead of flying off in one direction or the other."

"How do I do that?"

"I'm afraid you'll have to figure it out on your own. I've never given riding lessons to a cat before. Chimpanzees; yes, and even once a young gorilla, but not a cat; not a true four-legged creature. Think you can teach yourself how to balance?"

"I'll try my best," Kitten said.

"Is everyone ready?" the General called out. Seeing the tabby atop the mountain pony, she nodded in approval. "Come on, then!" Wolf took off at a healthy lope, the grizzly running at her side, and the great herd followed. The once-small patrol party, now an army of more than five hundred, was on its way.

CHAPTER FIVE

On the Move

"We're about to enter the third sector," the Haflinger told his passenger. "See that large group of tall pines just ahead of us? That's it—through those trees and down the hill."

"I hope we can stop and rest when we get there." Kitten's head was starting to droop. Though the pony showed no signs of fatigue other than a light coat of sweat after hours of steady trotting, the tabby was quite worn out. Riding was hard work for the feline, who had been constantly shifting his short little legs like a set of bent-knee pistons that had to move up and down to absorb the bounces of the equine's lively gait. "My legs hurt," the cat stated.

"We'll probably stop for eating and drinking."

"And naps, I hope."

With the General, First Horse, and Bear at its head, the army formed itself into a narrow column and began to enter the grove of pines. Kitten and Pony were directly behind the wolf, and the feline heard her sniff suddenly. "Halt!" the canid cried, and stood still; her troops coming to an immediate stop. The General sniffed the air again. "Fire; there was a fire. It's out now." She moved forward slowly, and the army followed at a careful walk.

As those at the column's head emerged from the pine grove, they saw what lay at the base of the hill, and stopped. In a small valley at the bottom of the grassy slope, a scene of complete devastation stretched out before them: blackened ground and charred tree stumps, smoldering piles of debris, once-clear streams now polluted by ash. The dreadful landscape was draped in mourning; wearing a pall of thick grey smoke that hung as a stinking fog in the still, heavy air.

The bear stood up on his hind legs, pointed his nose at the sky, and roared in wild fury. The hair along Wolf's spine rose up as she let out a deep-throated growl of rage. "Petroleum!" the canid snarled. "Smell the petroleum!"

"What does that mean?" Kitten whispered to the pony.

"It means this wasn't a natural fire—it was deliberately set. There would have been no stopping it, and likely no escape for those caught within its boundaries."

The feline flattened himself out along the Haflinger's spine. "Oh, no." He pressed his nose into the pony's sleek coat. "Awful, awful," he whimpered.

The canid sat down on her haunches. Her eyes, her beautiful topaz eyes; they had taken on a different light: an icy illumination. Staring straight ahead with a super-focused gaze that would have surely frozen the heart of any creature unfortunate enough to meet her look, the wolf sat so perfectly still that one might have thought her to be a statue. Slowly, a corner of her mouth drew back; then the upper lip was raised, and a stretch of deep-pink gum over the front teeth showed itself. On either side of the pink, pairs of lengthy snow-white fangs were bared as the wolf's jaws quivered with a rage too powerful to be contained within her body.

The General rose to her feet, threw her head back, and sent a blood-chilling howl into the sky. It was immediately answered by a howl of a different sort: a shrieking, violent wind leapt up and screamed through the valley in instant response to the lady's cry; shattering the awful stillness of the smoke-shrouded landscape. Wailing in furious harmony with the wolf, it gave physical expression to the canid's grief; snapping burnt tree stumps in half with its unrestrained force while sending charred debris flying high into the air.

Kitten dug his claws into the Haflinger's heavy coat; trying to avoid being blown from his mount's back as the powerful wind tossed heavy objects about. "Help!" he called out.

The wolf heard the tabby's cry. "Bear!" she shouted into the wind. "Get the cat!"

The grizzly turned and, in a quick grab, seized the kitten a second after he became airborne. Dropping down onto three legs, the bear held the tiny tiger close to his chest.

Wolf hung her head low and tried to relax, knowing it was the only way to make the wind stop. Closing her eyes, she struggled to calm down; breathing slowly and deeply. "Easy, easy," she whispered to herself.

As the canid relaxed, so did the violent wind; spinning down into bursts of fitful breezes that soon sputtered out into nothing. The air became still again, and all was quiet. The land that had once been alive with the happy music of singing birds and chattering animals was now deadly silent; a blackened landscape stripped naked of its former vitality.

Bear put Kitten down on the ground and rose to stand upright at his full height. Gazing down at the tragedy before him, he moaned. "Look at that—look at that perfect neat border where bright living greenery turns to dead black. It's horrifying how they can kill sweet moist vegetation with such efficiency."

"The Flöbbertigôbbet has his ways: petroleum fuel, flame throwers, trucks." Wolf's eyes closed, and she whimpered softly. "If only I'd known all the facts. If I had been here sooner, I could've done something. If only I had been here to direct a counterassault."

First Horse looked down at the General. "You can't be everywhere, ma'am. It's a big hemisphere."

Wolf's eyes were busily at work; surveying the still-smoking horizon. The filly's sensitive ears could hear the General's teeth clicking together: a sign that the canid, while appearing calm on the outside, was furious inside, and planning a hostile response. The equine knew better than to interrupt her superior's thoughts at such a time, and waited patiently for the leader to speak. She soon did. "We're going ahead. The fortress is only a few days off if we go in a straight line."

The wolf turned to address her troops. "It is my intention to march to the fortress," she announced in a clear voice. "It is likely that the land will be dead and burned all the way, with no food or clean water available. It will be an extremely difficult voyage. If any of you do not feel up to it, now is the time to turn back." The General waited, but not a single animal turned away. She looked down at the cat, who was lying on the ground at her feet. "Kitten—I can send you back, if you like. The pony can carry you to the emerald grove."

"No, ma'am. I came here to fight the Flöbbertigôbbet. I'm not going home until I've faced him."

"Very well." Wolf addressed her troops again. "We don't have much time. The enemy is probably planning another assault on our territory. There's lots of good grass here. Eat quickly, then we'll be on our way." She leaned down to put a word into the tabby's ear. "As there's nothing for you to eat, young fellow, you may as well use the time for a nap."

"Yes, ma'am." Kitten shut his eyes and tried to put himself to sleep; eventually succeeding at falling into exhausted slumber.

"Wake up." Wolf nudged the feline with her nose. "It's time to go."

"Oh." The cat leapt to his feet. "Ouch!"

"What is it?"

"I'm sorry, ma'am—my legs are very sore from riding the pony. I'm not used to the movement. I'll; I'll be okay." He took a step forward, and winced.

"Don't be excessively brave, son—you'll just end up crippled. Bear!"

"Yes, ma'am!"

"Kitten needs an easy ride until his legs have recovered."

"Yes, ma'am." The grizzly scooped up the little tiger and held him close to his chest.

"Thank you, sir."

"My pleasure." He dropped down onto three legs and turned his attention to his leader.

Wolf addressed her troops. "Does anyone need more grass? How about you, Bear—did you eat enough berries to keep you going for a good long while?"

"I ate every edible thing I could find, ma'am."

"Excellent." The General looked over the crowd of horses. Not a single equine was indicating a need for more grass, so the canid turned and faced the blackened horizon. "March on!" she ordered, and the army began to move forward at speed; the wolf at its head.

Kitten watched the ground fly past as he rested comfortably within the great paw of the grizzly. The tabby had never seen scorched earth before. "Bear," he asked, "will this land be dead forever?"

"It shall recover in time," the grizzly replied. "Seeds and roots far down in the ground are probably still alive, and when the rains come; I expect in the spring, we will see signs of plant life again. The streams might revive themselves eventually and run clear, flushing out the charcoal and soot along with the incendiary fuel the enemy used."

"I'm glad to hear that."

"The revival of the land is a small comfort when one considers the lives that will not be recovered: rabbits, woodchucks, beavers, deer, wolves, lynxes, and whatnot; not to mention any camels, chimpanzees, and elephants who were in the area delivering food for the carnivores. Only birds would've been able to escape the flames. With a natural fire set by lightning, most would have been able to flee in time, but that is not the case with a trap-fire set by the enemy. Countless lives were lost here."

"I guess that's why Wolf . . . that's why she lost her temper, so to speak, and made the awful wind."

"Yes. Our leader is the one most gifted at directing the currents of nature. When Wolf is pushed too far, nature is pushed as well. It's difficult for the General, I expect, when one considers the frequency and extent of the pain which the Flöbbertigôbbet inflicts on her. If the pain pushes her to lose her temper, she can accidentally damage portions of our territory."

Kitten looked to one side, then the other. He could see nothing but blackened ground and smoldering tree stumps. "Do you know how long it'll take us to get to the fortress? The General said it would be a few days. How many days make a few?"

"Well . . . for a fast-moving army like us, it'll probably take about four days."

"I see." The tabby tried not to think about the threat of prolonged emptiness in his stomach. To distract himself, he focused on a bigger subject: the enemy. "Does the Flöbbertigôbbet ever leave his fortress?"

"Not physically, no."

"What do you mean? He leaves it not physically?"

"The creature exists in a different sort of nature from the one you and I know. He isn't mortal."

"I've heard about that nonmortality business of his before," the tabby snorted, "and quite frankly, I don't believe it."

"You don't?"

"No! The Flöbbertigôbbet exists here in our physical reality, so I think he is basically as mortal as we are. I'm sure that so-called immortality of his is just an illusion he's milking for all it's worth."

"An illusion, eh? That's a radical notion." The bear nodded. "I must say I like it—I like it very much."

"I'm glad you do," the tabby said.

"So what's your plan, Kitten?"

"My plan?"

"You told the General you're not going home until you've faced the Flöbbertigôbbet. What are you going to do when you finally meet him?"

"I guess I'll cross that bridge when I come to it. Since I can't find anyone who can give me a precise description of his capabilities and physical appearance, making a plan as to how to deal with him would be a waste of time, wouldn't it? Unless you can give me a good description of him; can you?"

"No natural creature can do that. The ones who go inside the fortress to see him either die or emerge as members of his army."

"Terrific," Kitten growled. "Hey—what's up?"

Wolf had brought the army to a halt and was standing stock-still, watching the horizon. A soot-covered truck was there in the distance; growing larger as it bounced forward over the rough ground. "Bear—get the cat behind the troops!" the General ordered.

Raising her voice, she shouted at the army, "Wall formation; stand ready!" The mass of equine soldiers quickly formed themselves into a solid battle line of fight-ready flesh, ten horses deep and fifty wide.

The grizzly loped through the lines of quadrupeds and stationed himself behind them, placing the tabby on his left shoulder as he stood upright. "What's going on?" Kitten asked.

"I've seen this before. If the driver of the truck takes the bait and goes to ram the standing-wall formation, the horses will reorganize at the last possible moment, surrounding the thing behind and on both sides, and kick it to pieces. The rough ground slows down the truck, but not the horses; they can win."

"What if whoever is inside has flame throwers or something?"

"They won't have anything that can stop all five hundred horses."

The truck continued to move forward, then screeched to an abrupt halt a few hundred feet away. Wolf waited, not wanting her horses to expend precious energy on a galloping charge. The canid sat quietly, ears forward and alert, as the truck's powerful engine raced noisily in idle gear. There was a sudden crunching of metal against metal, and the truck spun around and raced off in the opposite direction. The General snorted softly. "Some of the greys are getting smarter, it seems!" she declared to her troops.

First Horse responded with an earsplitting neigh. "I'm sorry they turned back!" she cried. "It would have been a pleasure to reduce that damnable truck to a useless pile of shredded metal!"

"The greys drive, then," Kitten said to the grizzly. "I didn't think they could do that—I was just being sarcastic when I said they likely delivered that nasty trap in an SUV."

"They don't drive well, but they do manage to get around." Seeing the General step out into a trot, the grizzly followed in her footsteps, and the march resumed.

Four very difficult days had passed. No food, no water, no sleep, and constant hard exercise; the troops were worn out. Wolf, whose predatory constitution was made for long hunts on an empty stomach; she was in fine shape. The rest of the army, however, was exhausted from hunger and thirst. Horses are grazers; creatures meant to be almost constantly involved in the act of eating, and these equines were accustomed to a continuous supply of food. Bear came from a line of beasts who nibble nonstop as well; barring time spent in winter hibernation. Having to go on a super-active march with no food, water, or rest was very hard on the grizzly. And little Kitten, a growing babe in the habit of receiving rich Stilton and high-protein salmon several times a day between frequent naps: he was truly suffering.

Bear set the tabby down on the blackened ground and sighed. "I have to stop." His dragging feet could go no further.

First Horse came to a halt at the grizzly's side. Her eyes were half shut and her head hung low, its long silver-streaked forelock covering her face like a veil. "Ma'am; we need to rest."

The General sat down and looked into the red glow of the late afternoon sun, now in the process of setting behind a scorched hilltop. "We will stop for a bit, then."

First Horse bent her legs and lowered herself to the ground. As her head hit the burnt earth, black soot coated one side of her pale face. The equine was too tired to care about personal hygiene and closed her eyes, hoping to fall into the bliss of slumber.

Kitten flopped down in a heap. Charcoal ash floated up to darken the white fur of his throat and chin, but, like First Horse, the usually tidy cat was too exhausted to be concerned about things like cleanliness. Closing his eyes, he sighed, twitched, and was asleep in a short second.

Wolf stared into the setting sun: a shallow arch of gleaming deep-tangerine fire that blinked brightly behind the recumbent body of the hill before fading into nothingness. "We're headed straight for failure," she thought. "Without food and water, by the time we get to the fortress, we'll be so weak. We are facing utter failure. What was I thinking, to bring my troops into this wasteland? Everything covered with choking ash: if I were to raise a rainstorm in order to give my army something to drink, the water would be polluted as soon as it hit the ground. I can't expect horses to drink raindrops as they fall from above: equines need great quantities of water. What have I done?" The General gazed at the fading orange sky, and as she did so, her sharp eyes caught a movement in the distance—lights were coming out of the area where the sun had just disappeared.

The canid watched the blinking, bouncing collection of tiny sparks on the horizon. As the sparks moved closer, it became clear that they were a set of three pairs of bright headlights. Wolf waited, and heard a familiar engine noise. "It's Jean-Baptiste!" the General cried. Leaping to her feet, she wagged her tail.

First Horse raised her sooty head. "Jean-Baptiste?"

"He has the truck he always drives, and there are two other trucks with him. They have long cylindrical tanks on their beds. They look like petroleum trucks. Why would he bring petroleum?"

The three huge trucks lumbered slowly forward; moving with difficulty over the bumpy earth. When they came to within a hundred yards of the army, they stopped; engines idling. The headlights of the truck pulling the semitrailer were switched off and the vehicle moved gradually forward, stopping a short distance from the waiting wolf. The driver's-side door opened, and a young man dressed in blue jeans and a red-and-black plaid shirt jumped out; landing gracefully on sneaker-shod feet. "General!" the tall, slightly built fellow called out. Pushing his long brown hair back from his face, he smiled. "Hello!"

The General trotted forth to meet the visitor. "Jean-Baptiste—what are you doing so far beyond our border?"

"I saw what happened here; at least, I saw satellite images of it on my computer: a fire set by arsonists, a herd of horses moving towards the remains of it, a violent windstorm that erupted from the head of that herd when it arrived at the burned area, and the consequent straight-line progress of that herd, which is obviously heading for the fortress. I didn't have to be a genius to figure out what was going on."

"But why did you cross our border? What moved you to violate the treaty?"

"The satellite images showed the extent of the damage here. You'll be needing food and water, I expect."

"You mean those aren't petroleum trucks?"

"No, ma'am—that's fresh, clean water; enough for your army there. And my truck is filled with sacks of pellets for both carnivores and herbivores. I have the usual brown pellets for you, with green ones for the horses."

The wolf was silent as she considered the situation. She hated to compromise her position by erupting into an expression of the gratitude she felt, but the young man had clearly risked his life to bring supplies to her army. While it was unlikely that any natural animal would have troubled him or his fellow drivers, there were always the greys and their unpredictable assaults, and a large group of them might have set upon the three trucks with more ferocity than the small party of monsters had shown to the herd of five hundred horses. However, if the General showed her appreciation for Jean-Baptiste's courage and received the men kindly, she might be setting a precedent that would encourage future invasions of the hemisphere of which she was in charge.

"I understand your position, ma'am," Jean-Baptiste said. "Our visit here is being kept a secret. In fact, the time-consuming complications of hiding our actions are the reason we didn't get here sooner. Be assured that images of this meeting will not be broadcast on the evening news along with the glorious announcement that we got away with trespassing on natural soil. I have friends who have seen to it that the satellites overhead are currently suffering from 'unexplained' malfunctions. No one can see us."

"I see." Wolf nodded. "I thank you, then, for your help. You were right to suspect that we would be in need of food and water. My troops are in distress."

"Let's not waste time, then." Jean-Baptiste waved to the pair of waiting trucks, which moved closer to the herd and parked. Eight men jumped out of the two forward cabs and ran to the semitrailer. Moving quickly, they unloaded a quantity of large self-inflating wading pools and began to set them up. With eager horses waiting at the pools' edges, four of the men affixed hoses to the holding tanks of the trucks and began to dispense water as the others set to work unloading biodegradable sacks of feed pellets, which they set on the ground and slit open with knives.

Jean-Baptiste watched as Bear and Kitten ran to one of the open bags of brown pellets. "That's a real cute little tabby," he said. "I haven't seen one of those since I left home."

"He's from your world," the General said. "He came to fight the Flöbbertigôbbet."

"Oh! Ambitious cat, eh?"

"Unlike you, Jean-Baptiste, he didn't come here to escape an unpleasant situation. He's a tough little fellow. Sadly out of shape, perhaps, but still a good little fighter."

"I'm sick of fighting. I never want to fight again."

"If you were truly sick of fighting, you wouldn't have risked your life to come help me and my troops."

"Maybe . . ." Jean-Baptiste narrowed his gentle brown eyes. "Maybe I'm just sick of fighting certain things." Stuffing his work-roughened hands into the deep pockets of his loose jeans, he smiled. "Now, this— seeing your wonderful army of fabulous fighting horses close up—that's something I could never get sick of." The young man looked down at the wolf. "Aren't you going to drink with them?"

"I'm built for hardship, son. I can wait until my troops have had their fill."

"They don't make generals like you in my world, ma'am; at least, not anymore."

"I'm not the perfect officer you might believe me to be, Jean-Baptiste. I'm an overemotional fool, risking the lives of my army in an assault on the Flöbbertigôbbet when I know we can't beat him. Even if we kill every soldier he sends out against us, he'll manage to keep himself safe and alive; if you want to call what he is 'alive.'"

"Still . . . if you reduce the size of his army, you'll slow him down."

"'Slow him down': hardly an achievement I would describe as a glorious victory."

"Sometimes one has to settle for what one can get."

The wolf looked up at the young man. "How goes the work of the priests?"

"The same as always, ma'am. They build bigger churches and temples, claiming that if they can bring enough people into their congregations, they'll be able to overcome the Flöbbertigôbbet with prayers. As you already know, they've been using the same war plan for centuries with no results whatsoever. At least, there are no results that anyone can plainly see."

"Is the conservative wing still claiming that animals are inferior to humans, and that our control of the weather and whatnot is a form of evil witchcraft?"

"You betcha, ma'am."

The canid shook her head. "I thank the god of the wolves that we no longer have to share the same space as those twisted creatures."

"And I thank the same god that our scientists are on your side so those conservative maniacs can't make any progress with the hideous bombs they're lobbying for." Jean-Baptiste bent down to address the wolf in a soft voice. "I wish you'd drink something, ma'am. I'm sure you're thirsty."

"Yes, I am. But I can wait a bit longer. There are still a few horses who haven't had a turn at the water." The General looked up at her human friend. "When we're finished drinking, will you please remove the plastic ponds?"

"They're wading pools, designed for children to splash around in." The young man stood upright again. "Don't worry, ma'am; we'll take them back with us. I know the terms of the treaty well: the people had to remove all buildings, roads, and non-biodegradable man-made materials from your area. But perhaps; you will be returning from the fortress, correct?"

"I believe now that we are fed and watered, we shall prevail, son. We might not enjoy a great victory, but we will not be utterly defeated."

"Perhaps it would be best if we left the pools for a little while. Your troops will be needing something to drink on the way back."

Wolf looked down at the ground, her brow furrowed.

"I know you hate the idea of all that stuff lying about here, ma'am, but when the treaty was made, no one from your side had any idea that the Flöbbertigôbbet would lay waste to such a large area that you'd be needing an artificial water supply."

The General remained silent.

"We won't hang around here, I promise. I'll go home and watch the satellite images on my computer, and when I see that your army has left the fortress and passed through this area again, I'll come and retrieve the pools. I still have access to the satellite feeds, though no one else does."

"Very well." The canid nodded. "Please don't think I'm not appreciative of your help."

"No need to explain, ma'am—I understand your position perfectly."

"Thank you." The wolf stepped forward. "The last horse has been watered—I can drink now."

"We'll be on our way, General. Come on, guys!" Jean-Baptiste shouted to his associates. The men detached themselves from the crowd of horses with whom they had been chatting and headed toward their trucks.

The General bobbed her nose at the group of eight as they passed her. "Thank you, gentlemen. We are in your debt."

"It's our pleasure, ma'am," one of the men said. "It was an honor to be here."

The trucks' engines roared to life, and the big vehicles were driven off. Wolf drank and drank, then went to a bag of brown pellets and filled her stomach with a hefty portion. Lying down on the charred ground, she addressed her waiting troops. "Let's have a bit of rest, now. Kitten!" The tabby ran to his friend's side. "Here—curl up with me. If you sleep next to that huge bear, he might accidentally roll over on top of you, and you would be done for. We don't want that to happen, do we?"

"No, ma'am!" The little tiger curled up against the soft fur of the canid's stomach and began to purr heartily.

The General's eyes were bright with appreciation. "My pups were the loves of my life," she said to the cat. "No one will ever take a place above them in my heart but, marvelous as they were, they couldn't purr. I must say, it's quite charming."

"Thank you. I . . ." The feline didn't finish the phrase he had started, overcome by heavy slumber.

Wolf lowered her head and fell into sleep, her legs bent protectively about her small friend. The grizzly flopped down onto the ground with a heavy thud and almost instantly let loose with a burst of loud snoring. First Horse reclined near the great bear, but kept her head and shoulders upright in order to keep an alert vigil over the landscape. The rest of the herd followed Bear's lead, giving in to sleep as the second-in-command kept watch.

●———●—●—●—●—●—●—●

First Horse opened her eyes, feeling the nudge of a canine nose against her cheek. A young bay stallion had relieved her at sentry duty a short time earlier, and the filly was enjoying a very sound slumber. Wolf, however, had decided that all had had enough rest. "It's time to move on," the canid told the equine. "Dawn will arrive in a few hours, and I want to be at the fortress before the sun rises—as you know, the energy level of the greys is lowest in the early morning. Just a moment for eating and drinking, then we have to be off."

The filly jumped up and let out a full-throated whinny. "Attention!" First Horse cried. "Up and ready! We're leaving soon, so have at the water and pellets one last time!"

Kitten had been roused when Wolf rose from her sleep, and was already filling his stomach with pellets. Bear broke out of his snoring slumber to join the feline and began to gobble greedily at the carnivore feed.

"This protein stuff seems to hold me for longer than the green pellets," the grizzly said.

"Must be nice, being an omnivore." Kitten swallowed a well-chewed mouthful of the crunchy food. "You have more choices than I do."

"Uh, huh." Bear nodded and scooped up another pawful of pellets, throwing them into his open mouth. Swallowing, he looked down at the tabby. "You want to come along with me again?"

"I'd be happy to ride with you a little while longer, sir."

"There." The grizzly stopped and stood upright. The coming dawn's first gentle light was beginning to show itself. "See those tall white poles? That's our edge of the border."

"Your edge?" Kitten peeked out from between the bear's long curved claws.

"Yes. We have our border—the white poles—then there's a neutral territory, so to speak, that's a strip about a mile wide, then the human hemisphere has its border."

The little tiger looked down the gentle slope of the blackened hill. Set into the level ground at its base was an orderly line of tall, snowy-white marble columns that marched along the earth as far as the eye could see, with enough room between them to allow adult elephants to pass easily through any point of the symbolic barrier. Beyond the columns, the land was unburnt; green with grass, bushes, and trees. If not for the thick mass of the forest, Kitten might have been able to see the wall that contained humanity's hemisphere.

Bear dropped back down onto three legs and strode forward with his tiny passenger, following the path of the wolf who trotted ahead to the row of columns. "Where's the fortress?" Kitten asked.

"It's in the neutral strip," the grizzly replied. "I've never actually seen it—my mother taught me its location so I'd know to stay away from there."

"I had imagined it would be a huge towering thing that one could see for miles around. If it can be hidden within these trees, it must be fairly small."

"That's an illusion. The . . . the . . ." Being in close proximity to the fortress was an experience which was having a profound effect on Kitten's friend. For thousands of years, long before the border's hemispheric division had come into being, campaigns of hideous oppression had been sent forth from the ruling resident of the stronghold. Bear had lost many relatives and friends to the gruesome games played by the beast that resided within, and the memories of those deaths were rising up now to taunt him. Knowing the painful emotions could cause him to lose his sense, the grizzly fought to keep them at bay. He searched for the line of thought he had almost lost, and resumed his sentence. "The Flöbbertigôbbet rejoices in deception. The fortress is large, as you suspected. He puts up a sort of screen that makes the structure

133

invisible until one gets fairly close to it. This no longer fools any of the residents of our hemisphere, but he keeps the supernatural screen up just; just because he likes to."

Wolf stepped onto the green grass that met the blackened edge of her land. "Troops—halt!"

"Shouldn't she be more quiet?" Kitten asked the bear in a cautious whisper.

The grizzly stopped, set down the kitten, and stood upright. "It wouldn't do any good—the Flöbbertigôbbet knows we're here."

"He isn't some awful omniscient thing, is he?"

"He knows more than we'd like him to know."

"Great," Kitten growled.

The General turned to address her army. "Unless the Flöbbertigôbbet has recently managed to acquire new soldiers and technologies from the human side, which I'm fairly certain he has not, we will prevail. I've been tallying up informed estimates of how many of his greys are out and about in our hemisphere, and I believe that he does not have nearly enough fighters here in his stronghold to overwhelm our present numbers. In fact, there is a distinct possibility that this will turn into a beleaguerment; not hand-to-hand combat. There is plenty of grass and water at hand, so we can survive the inflicting of a very long siege." Wolf looked down at Kitten, who was seated on the ground beside the grizzly. "I know where to find carnivore pellets in this area, son; don't worry."

The tabby nodded.

The General addressed her troops again. "As you know, there is only one way in or out of the fortress. We will station ourselves in a large mass at the main gate, with groups of sentries posted at intervals along the perimeter of the moat to watch for anyone who might attempt to exit from a window. Such an exit would likely be suicide, since the greys do not swim well and would surely drown in the moat, but still, we must keep an eye out just in case." Wolf looked over her troops. "Are there any questions?"

"Ma'am!" Kitten waved his twisted front paw.

"Yes?"

"Someone told me that the increased aggression in the third sector had something to do with me. Is that true?"

"I have heard the rumor. Whether or not it is true, I don't know. Such information would probably have originated from the enemy camp, so its veracity is questionable."

"I see."

"Are there any other questions?" There were none. "To the gate, then!" Wolf cried.

The army entered the forest. Kitten, trotting forward on the grassy earth, was happy to be in a place of shade and living greenery. The past days spent in the scorched, dead wasteland had been miserable indeed, and it was delightful to once again see sunlight glowing through the lush canopies of healthy trees. The one negative note was the total absence of animal life: no furry chipmunks scurrying up and down oak trunks, no chirping birds flitting about, not even the humming of insects was to be heard.

The column had gone only a short distance through the woods before Wolf brought the army to a halt. "There it is," she said to the tabby. "That's the fortress." The General pointed her left forepaw to indicate an opening between two slender birch trees. An impressive structure had become visible from that viewpoint.

Kitten sat down abruptly, surprised. "It's beautiful!" A cream-colored fairy-tale castle rose up from the forest floor; as pretty as a wedding cake with its corkscrew tiers of elegant masonry climbing up tall towers whose arched windows should have held golden-haired princesses waiting for courageous noblemen to climb up their braided locks. "Holy moly! It's a Rapunzel; no, it's a Cinderella castle!"

"Cinderella?"

"It's a happy-ending children's story I heard somewhere."

"That's no happy ending there. That's the home of the Most Evil."

"How can there be evil in there? It's so pretty!"

"Pretty? So are the plants whose beautiful sweet-smelling flowers lure insects into a sticky trap so they can be eaten alive. Beauty is no indication of goodness."

"I guess."

"Would you like to know how many animals have gone into that pretty castle to meet with a death too horrible to describe?"

"No; thank you, ma'am."

The General turned to First Horse. "Pick some sentries to station round the moat, and have the rest of the army come with me to the entrance, where we shall wait. Battle or siege—that decision will be made by the enemy. I am certain he will choose the latter."

"Yes, ma'am." First Horse trotted into the herd.

"It's so frustrating," Wolf said to the little feline. "To know that the source of all evil in our hemisphere is there inside those walls, and there is nothing we can do to stop him. We've tried, and tried, and nothing but death has come from our efforts: death, or the total corruption of those who entered with the hope of overcoming him."

"Won't the siege accomplish something?"

"The Flöbbertigôbbet's soldiers—the greys—who are trapped inside the fortress will be deprived of the live food they need to survive. They'll either starve to death in there or try to fight their way out, in which case we will overcome them. But the Flöbbertigôbbet: he can't be starved." Wolf observed that the sentries had been chosen and were heading for their assigned posts. "Come, son—wait with me."

The tabby and canid walked to the edge of the wooden drawbridge, which was in its lowered position, and the troops followed. "Make yourselves comfortable," the wolf told her soldiers. "Stay alert, of course, but go ahead and lie down, or graze if you wish." The army spread itself out before the castle's entrance; some horses nibbling at green grass, others reclining. The grizzly began to pick at a bush covered with sweet red berries.

Wolf settled down onto the ground, Kitten at her side, and gazed through the entryway of the fortification. The heavy iron grate that protected the interior court of the castle was down; its dagger-like ends firmly set into the receiving holes of the entrance's metal threshold. The little tiger stared ahead in fascination, trying to see signs of life inside the fortress. At the moment, there was nothing visible but the flagstone pavement of a spacious courtyard. The tabby glanced to his right, where sat a low barrier of stones and mortar that ran all the way around the castle, excepting the opening for the drawbridge. Leaping onto the barrier's top, the feline looked down and saw an extremely deep moat; its murky waters sitting stagnant a considerable distance down from the wall's top.

Gazing into the chasm-like depths of the protective ditch, which seemed more like a narrow canyon than a constructed work, Kitten started to feel dizzy, and jumped off the wall and back onto steady solid earth. Returning to Wolf's side, he sat back on his haunches and stared ahead into the empty courtyard. "You say the Flöbbertigôbbet can't be starved. Why is that?"

"Because he doesn't need to eat."

"Are you certain about that?"

"I'm fairly certain. We've besieged this castle before, and while his monsters have come out starved and desperate, he's never shown his face."

"Maybe he has a personal food supply that has never been depleted."

"That's possible, I suppose; however, as far as we know, he simply does not eat. He isn't like you and me, or even like his horrible greys."

Kitten gazed at the grate barring the entrance, his eyes thoughtful. "You know, that wouldn't be impossible to break down. You could use; I'll bet elephants could bend the bars apart if they tried hard enough. Or small animals: ones my size could fit through the spaces between the iron rods and get inside."

"It would be pointless to go inside, son. As I have said before, the Flöbbertigôbbet cannot be killed by mere mortals like ourselves. The best we can do is take on his soldiers."

"I'm getting tired of hearing that. I just don't buy it!"

The canid sighed. "Kitten . . ." She leapt to her feet. "Kitten—no!"

The tiny tiger had bolted forward; a flying blur of black stripes and silver fur galloping straight for the grate. The General flew after him, but the tabby had the advantage of surprise and beat her to his goal by a cat's length. Springing easily through the narrow space between two heavy bars, he turned and faced his distressed friend, who could not have fit through the grate if she had been half her present size.

Wolf put her nose between the bars. "Kitten, please: come back. If you go any further, I'll never see you again! You don't know what goes on in there! Please!"

"I'm sorry, ma'am." Kitten shook his head. "I came here to fight the Flöbbertigôbbet, not his monsters. I want to see him face to face."

"This way is suicide!"

"I have to do this, ma'am." The tabby looked into the pleading eyes of the canid and felt a terrible squeezing at his heart that was far too much like the pain he had felt when his new owner took him away from his mother. This wolf had become his surrogate parent, and it was agonizing for the little feline to see the grief in her eyes. "I love you, Wolf, and I will be back. Wait for me." Kitten turned and walked away, trying to close his ears to the anguished howl that followed him.

The General's expression of mourning ended as the tabby vanished from her line of sight. Leaving the grate, she trotted back to her post at the end of the drawbridge and settled down on the grass. Closing her eyes, she began a mental scan of her hemisphere; searching far and wide for the presence of extraordinary soldiers: elephants, rhinoceroses, bulls, eagles, falcons, tigers, lions, panthers, boa constrictors, pythons, grizzlies, wolves—anyone who could fight, and fight well.

CHAPTER SIX

The Meeting

Kitten darted to his left; hugging the wall of the courtyard as he stole into enemy territory. An arched entryway was nearby, and he dashed through it; hoping the darkness inside would hide him. Seeing a low wooden table, he ran and hid under it; using the squat shelter as a cave in which to huddle in relative safety as he surveyed his new surroundings.

He sat motionless; ears forward and alert as he listened carefully for any sound which might betray the presence of a dangerous foe. All seemed quiet. Kitten turned his head ever so slowly from side to side as he scanned the territory; unwilling to make any sudden, large movements which might attract attention from a lurking predator. He could hear nothing, and saw no signs of anything living as he looked over what he could see of the large library in which he had found himself.

"This looks very much like my Lady's house," he thought. "This Oriental carpet resembles the old one in her library. And that antique stool at the window: it looks exactly like the one I was standing on as I talked with Dove." The nervous feline began to blink one eye. "This isn't right. It's true that I haven't been in a great many houses in my short life and I am not an expert on interior decoration, but I do know that different people aren't supposed to have identical furnishings. That stool is a perfect copy of my Lady's; I'm certain of it, and so is the carpet."

Kitten crept out from under the table and made a mad bolting dash to a nearby couch. Wriggling under it, he looked at the interior structure of the piece. "Another exact copy," he thought. "I've spent a lot of time under my Lady's couch. Right over there, in that corner, there should be a loose spring." He scuttled over to the corner and checked. "Yup—there it is." The feline chewed his lower lip in consternation. "This is most perplexing. Have I gone back home? Was Wolf wrong about what goes on in here? Maybe; maybe that grate I went through is another kind of Door, and I've gone back to my Lady's library again." The tabby pondered the situation. "Bear said that the Flöbbertigôbbet delights in deception. This must be a deception. It would be a good way to trick me into letting down my guard, wouldn't it—making me think I'm back in my safe sweet home. Ha! I'm not buying it!"

"Puss-puss-puss!" a female voice called.

The tabby started in surprise, bumping his head against one of the supporting boards of the couch. "Sounds just like the housekeeper," he thought. "But there's no way I'm going to fall for that!"

A pair of plump pink hands set a plate down on the floor next to the sofa: gold-rimmed Sèvres porcelain, bearing aromatic chunks of blue-veined Stilton.

"Oh." Kitten sniffed the air with his super-sensitive nose. "Oh, that smells so good! Mellow and creamy; a first-rate cheese aged to absolute perfection. Oh, that smells delightful." He stared longingly at the plate, which sat about two inches from the edge of the couch. "Maybe I can reach out there to grab a bit without exposing too much of myself." Creeping forward on his stomach, the cat moved closer to the plate. In a sudden lightning flash, one paw shot out and swiped at the Stilton; grabbing a hefty portion.

Backing away from the sofa's edge, he huddled in the dark and nibbled happily at his cheese-covered foot. "Ummm," he murmured; lost in ecstasy, "ummm: that's so good." Licking his forepaw clean, he looked at the chunks remaining on the plate. "Curious—I'm still just as hungry as I was before. That much rich food would usually make a dent in my appetite, but I feel like I didn't eat anything at all. Well, maybe I need more."

He crept forward to approach the dish again, but it was pulled away by the pink hands; left in a spot about a foot away from the couch. "Oh, dear: my arm isn't that long. If I want more, I'll have to expose myself." The tabby considered this briefly. "I'm fairly certain that isn't my Lady's real housekeeper. There's one good way to find out for sure." He broke out of his silent thoughts and shouted, "Push the plate under the couch!"

"No, no, Kitten," the alleged housekeeper replied. "You must be a good boy and come out for it."

"Gotcha!" the tabby cried. "If you were really my Lady's housekeeper, you wouldn't have understood what I said!"

A hearty chuckle was heard from above. "I gave it my best shot," a male voice said.

"Your best shot wasn't good enough," Kitten retorted. "Try again!"

"I don't want to fire off salvos at you," the voice responded. "Can't we be friends?"

"Friends? No way!"

"Why? What have you got against me?"

"For one thing, I don't know who you are."

"I am the prince of this castle."

"I see. Then you are the prince of everything horrible."

"What gave you that idea?"

"The General gave me that idea."

"Wolf is a wonderful creature, but she is wrong. She's never been inside my castle; she's never met or even seen me. How can she know who and what I am?"

"I will not find fault with her, sir. She has protected and cared for me since I arrived in this strange world, and I go by what she says."

"If you were as faithful to her as you claim to be, you wouldn't have entered here."

"I made a promise to someone before I met her, and I cannot throw it aside. I'm sure she understands why I did what I did."

"What you are doing is cowering under a sofa like a frightened child. Come out and see me!"

"No!"

"Little cat: surely an intelligent fellow like you must realize that I have been trying to get you out from under that couch using the most gentle means at my disposal. If I were truly the dreadful beast you believe me to be, the ruler of the grey monsters, as the rumors

144

say, I could use them to force you out from under that piece of furniture."

"Then use force!" the tabby cried. "I will fight you to the death!"

There was a loud sigh. "This is a very stubborn feline."

"Damned straight," the tiny tiger muttered.

"Correct me if I'm wrong," the voice said.

"Yes?"

"You came here because you made a vow to fight me: correct?"

"Yes."

"Is hiding under a couch in keeping with that vow?"

Kitten growled briefly. "No." Creeping forward, he poked his head out from under the edge of the sofa and looked up.

Seated in a red-velvet wing chair opposite the couch was a dark-haired man of pleasing visage. Clad in a well-cut suit of fine black wool tailored to perfectly fit his slender athletic form, he could have been one of the handsome foreign princes who sometimes visited the Lady of Kitten's house. He appeared to be no more than thirty years of age, judging from his fresh complexion. No worry lines creased the ivory skin of his smooth forehead, and his innocent brown eyes had the look of one who was living a life filled with joy. He seemed, somehow, to be perfect.

The prince smiled at the little tiger. "Hello, young cat."

Kitten looked warily at the man. His ears flattened back against his head, betraying his deep distrust of the apparent paragon before him.

"Aren't you going to return my greeting? You don't wish to be rude, do you?"

"I don't believe this to be a situation in which etiquette is a truly serious concern," the tabby sniped.

"Have I been discourteous to you?"

Kitten continued to stare in silence.

"I must have been remiss in my manners, somehow. This negative response of yours must be my fault." The man frowned. "Would you like more Stilton?"

"I'm fine, thanks."

The prince smiled again. "How about a bit of poached salmon? I can have my chef whip some up in no time at all."

"Your food: the cheese you just gave me was, well; empty. It tasted good in my mouth, but it did nothing for my stomach. I expect any salmon you might offer would be just as unsatisfying."

"Perhaps the food here isn't suited for a foreign belly like yours."

Kitten snorted. "Yeah, right."

The Flöbbertigôbbet raised an elegant dark eyebrow. "Breaking through the concrete wall of your prejudice is going to be quite a task for me, isn't it?"

"Prejudiced? Me?"

"Yes, you! You have never met me before, yet you seem to think that you know my character quite well based on what others have told you. You are judging me on hearsay! Is that fair?"

Kitten closed his eyes and considered the man's words. "Well." He opened his eyes and looked at the prince. "My personal code of ethics does not allow me to do such a thing with a completely clear conscience."

"Have you become such a slave to compromise, then, that you're willing to ignore that code of ethics and leap into a life of uncivilized behavior?"

"No." The tabby squirmed; made very uncomfortable by the decision he felt forced to make. "If I am to be a noble cat, and not a savage, I must treat you with respect until you have shown that you do not deserve it." The cat crept out from under the sofa and leapt up onto the low table that sat between the couch and the velvet wing chair. Looking up at the pleasing face of the man, the feline bobbed his nose slightly. "I'm sorry, sir, that I was so rude."

"You're forgiven, young cat."

"You may call me 'Kitten': that is how I am known."

"Thank you, Kitten." The Flöbbertigôbbet bowed his head. "You may call me 'Prince.' That is how I am known to my friends."

"Very well, Prince."

"Speaking of friends, where have yours gone?"

"What do you mean?"

"As soon as you came into this room, the gang; I mean, the army outside left."

"They're gone?"

"Come with me—I'll show you." The prince left his chair and walked to a set of portable wooden steps; a small staircase on wheels that could be used to reach the highest shelves of the library. "I'll move this to the window so you can get a clear view." He pushed the apparatus to a tall window and climbed to its top platform; Kitten following at his heels. "Can you see out?" he asked the cat.

The tabby raised himself up to put his front paws onto the lowest safety rail of the platform and looked out. "I can see," he said quietly, his heart sinking down into the pit of his stomach.

Not a single animal stirred outside the moat barrier; there were only bushes, trees, and horse-trampled grass. A half-eaten bunch of red berries lay on the ground in the spot where the grizzly had flopped down to enjoy a snack. "She didn't wait for me," Kitten whispered. "I asked her to wait. I told her that I loved her and I asked her to wait."

"Did she say that she loved you?"

"No."

"Did she say that she would wait?"

"No. She just howled."

"A wolf is a complicated creature. A howl can mean anything."

"I thought it meant . . . I guess I didn't know what it meant." Kitten closed his eyes and flopped down on the wooden platform; deepest despair overwhelming him.

"Poor Kitten." The Flöbbertigôbbet reached down and gently picked up the tiny tiger. Cuddling the grief-stricken cat against his chest, he stroked the little striped head. "It will be all right, small fellow. I will be your friend, and a very good friend indeed. I have a room all ready for you. There are fun toys and soft cushions for you, tasty morsels to eat, and wonderful new friends; yes, marvelous new friends—friends who won't abandon you when things get tough." The prince carried the tabby down the portable staircase and stepped onto the carpet. "I'll take you to your private chamber, and we'll give you a nice brunch."

After the pair left the room and began to proceed along a mahogany-paneled corridor, the bookshelves and furnishings of the library faded behind them; dissolving into a greenish mist. The pretty carpets and marble floor vanished, taking the plate of cheese with them, and a boiling, evil-smelling bog was revealed. A second later, the handsome leaded-glass windows disappeared as well, and were replaced by solid walls of mildewed, moisture-sweating stone.

●—●—●—●—●—●—●—●

Kitten turned over and put his front paws on the outer edge of his circular green-velvet cat bed. "Would you like some more sausage?" the pretty young maid asked.

The tabby looked at the silver plate the blue-eyed blonde was holding as she knelt before him. "Just what kind of meat is that, anyway?" he asked.

"A fine carnivore such as yourself needn't be concerned with such things, sir," the girl replied. "And after what your friends did to you, it would serve them right if you were eating one of them."

Kitten's amber eyes grew very black, and the right one began to blink repeatedly. "Eat the bloody sausage yourself, woman! I will have no more of it."

The girl stood upright, and seized one of the fat brown tubes of meat. "Whatever you say, sir." Biting a chunk off, she smiled as a bit of juice dribbled down her chin. "It's very tasty, sir. I don't know why you don't want any more."

The tabby hissed. "Go away!" he shouted, and hissed again.

"Yes, sir!" The blonde spun round and made a quick beeline for the door, slamming it shut as her shiny black-patent pumps hit the white marble floor of the hallway.

Kitten sighed. "This world is awful. Everyone turns out to be, well, not what I thought they were; something else entirely and usually something worse, except for the Flöbbertigôbbet, who doesn't seem to be nearly as bad as everyone told me he was. I can't believe that Wolf left me here, and Bear, too: how could they all go like that? I love Wolf; I trusted her, and she left me behind. I guess she decided I was expendable: someone to be sacrificed. She seemed like such a wonderful creature, though; an animal who would never do anything wrong ever. Maybe abandoning me wasn't the wrong thing to do; maybe she had a good reason for leaving. And maybe she didn't; maybe I was wrong about her. I surely do make a great many mistakes. Well, now that I've apparently been abandoned by those whom I trusted, it seems the prince is the only option left to me. He doesn't want to fight me, which surprises me. I don't feel certain about who he is now; I don't feel certain about anything at all, except that it is probably better for me to go back home where things are comfortable and predictable. I wonder if the prince might show me the way back to England? Maybe he can return me to the emerald grove somehow."

There was a knock at the door. "Who is it?" the tabby shouted.

"It's the prince, Kitten."

"Good," the feline muttered. "I'll see if he can get me out of this horrible place." Raising his voice, he called, "Come in!"

The Flöbbertigôbbet opened the door a crack and put his head round the edge. "Are you sure it's all right? Venetia said you're in a bit of a mood—don't want to eat your brunch." The prince came into the room and closed the door behind him. Kneeling down before the cat, he looked into the feline's eyes with concern.

"She wouldn't tell me exactly what the sausage is made of, though she did imply that it might be someone I used to know."

"Oh, no; that's terrible! I'm sorry—so very sorry. Venetia is a new employee: she's only been working here for two days. I had no idea she could be so cruel. I will have her discharged immediately!"

"So . . . what is the sausage made of?"

"It's plant protein, like the pellets you were eating in the wild."

"It tasted like meat to me."

"I have a very good chef—he can do magic in the kitchen."

"I see."

"Are you enjoying the accommodations? Do you like your room?"

"I'm getting claustrophobic."

"Why? This is a huge chamber I've given you. It's the biggest room in the castle."

"I can't see out the windows—they're high up, they don't have sills wide enough for me to perch on, and there's no tall furniture near them that I can climb onto. Cats need to look out windows—it's very important to us."

"Oh." The prince surveyed the room. "You're right —I hadn't thought of that. And all the bits of furniture in here are so small that they won't hold you up high enough to see out the windows even if I move them around for you." The Flöbbertigôbbet fingered his clean-shaven chin. "I'll have to talk to my housekeeper about getting some bigger pieces up here. Would that make you happy?"

"Well, it would make me feel better, but it wouldn't make me happy."

"What would make you happy?"

"I want to go back to England. I want to go home."

"Well, I suppose, if it's really important to you, that could be managed."

"It could?" Kitten leapt to his feet. "I can go home?"

"Certainly. I'll have to make some arrangements, of course. Let's see," the prince closed his eyes for a moment, "my best driver is out of the area right now, and he has the only vehicle capable of making the trip. He should be back in a few days, though. Would you like to go when he returns?"

"Yes! Thank you, Prince!"

"You're welcome." The man stroked the happy feline's crooked spine. "I've been thinking," he said.

"What?" Kitten purred as the gentle hand caressed him.

"I couldn't help noticing that you have several, um; deformities."

The cat stiffened.

"What—did I say something wrong?"

The tabby backed away from the prince's hand. "I am not deformed!"

"Now, now, puss—let's be honest. You have a crooked spine, your tail is curled up and rigid, and your front left paw: the bones and pads are all wrong."

Kitten's eyes grew dark; their pupils huge and black. Memories of his brothers and sisters began to surface; their cruel taunting words and teasing. 'Crooked cat, crooked cat, crooked cat!' they loved to shout at him. Lady and Dove, however, had never even mentioned his twisted tail, funny paw, and crooked spine; neither had any of the animals in this world.

The tabby returned to his bed and curled up, glaring at the man before him.

"I want to help you," the prince said. "I have certain powers; I can heal the sick."

"I'm not sick!" the tiny tiger snarled.

"But surely those deformities make life difficult for you."

"Not at all. My curled-up tail is unique and quite fine, I think. My spine is not a problem; in fact, it gives a nice sort of arrogant strut to my walk. And the paw pads which you say are all wrong actually give me an enhanced dexterity which most cats do not possess."

"Then you don't want to be healed?"

"No."

"I see. As you wish, little fellow." The prince stood and looked down at the cat.

"Sir?" Kitten decided to forget the insult. The Flöbbertigôbbet meant well, after all. "Can I get my bigger furniture soon so that I may look out the windows while I am in here, please?"

"I'll see to it straightaway, Kitten." The prince bowed. As he headed for the door, the tabby rose and tried to exit with him. The Flöbbertigôbbet stopped at the threshold; his hand on the crystal knob. "We're spraying for insects today. It would be best if you stayed in this room where there won't be any poison floating about."

Kitten looked up at the man's kindly brown eyes. "Very well, sir." Backing away, the cat watched as the smiling prince left the room, closing the door behind him.

The tabby sat quiet and still in his bed all through the day, patiently waiting for someone to bring his furniture. Shortly before twilight, there was a knock on the door, and an elderly woman entered; a silver plate of sausage in her hand. "Here's your dinner, sir." She placed the dish on the floor before the cat.

Kitten looked at her with pleading eyes. "Ma'am: where's my furniture?"

"Furniture?"

"I'm supposed to be getting something to climb onto, please, so that I may look out the window. Cats need to look out windows: it's very important to us."

"I don't know anything about that, sir." The woman shrugged and turned away.

"Is the poison spraying over? Can I go out into the hallway now?"

The maid did not respond, slamming the door shut behind her as she left.

Kitten stared at the plate of food. "Oh, dear." His claws dug deep into the cushioned velvet of the bed as his tension level began to rise. "This does not look good. The Flöbbertigôbbet said he would take care of the furniture matter straightaway, but he seems to have forgotten about it. I suppose, being a prince, he has a lot of important matters on his mind and can't be bothered with the problems of a cat." The tabby blinked. "Oh, dear. If I don't get a look at the outside fairly soon, I will go mad, I think."

He looked round the room the prince had given him: a large gold-painted chamber occupying a generous corner of the second floor of the castle. Windows were set at regular intervals along the two outside walls; all of their sills a good four feet up from the floor. Kitten looked at the furnishings of the room: low tables and soft cushions scattered randomly about on a polished hardwood floor. Here and there were toys: fake mice, feathers tied to long sticks, balls that could be rolled around inside the fat plastic wheels which held them. "There's no way I can push those little things together into a mountain big and solid enough that I can climb up onto it to look out. There seems to be no easy solution. Well; there's only one thing I can do to stave off impending madness—I'll jump up and hang on."

Kitten rose from his bed and went to a window. After crouching down and wiggling about to gather his strength, he fired himself off into a great flying vertical

155

leap and used his sharp claws to grab onto the wood of the narrow sill. Pulling himself up high enough to see, he peered through the glass. Shocked by what he saw, he lost his grip and fell onto the floor.

A group of four equine sentries was standing watch outside the moat wall. Kitten had caught a glimpse of two large blood bays, a skinny black Thoroughbred type, and one of the Haflingers. "They didn't all leave, then!" he whispered.

He sprinted to the other wall to get a different view. Crouching and springing into another vertical leap, he clung to the edge of the sill and, hanging there, pulled his head up to look out this front window. Arranged in a tight mass before the castle was the great army of horses, the sleeping grizzly, and Wolf. The canid was at her post at the end of the drawbridge, staring through the grate.

Kitten was having trouble holding this difficult position and soon lost his grip. Falling to the floor, he collapsed on his stomach and lay there, breathing rapidly with excitement. "So—I was deceived. I was stupid, emotional, insecure, and faithless, and I allowed myself to be deceived. What was I thinking? If the Flöbbertigôbbet could supernaturally impersonate an English housekeeper and reproduce my Lady's furniture and cheese, which he surely did, he could certainly have made it seem that there was no one in front of the castle when there were in fact over five hundred bodies out there! How could I have been so stupid?"

The cat's practical nature jumped into play. "There's no point in beating myself to death over a mistake. It's time to plan a proper reaction to the

156

situation. Now—what shall I do? Shall I fight the Flöbbertigôbbet, as I vowed to, or should I try to escape?" He nibbled at his lopsided front paw as he pondered the situation. "If I leap onto the prince's head, it's a fair bet he'll pull me off and there won't be a fine First Horse here to rescue me. No, a frontal attack would be quite stupid at this time; downright suicidal. I would say escape is at present my only option. But how am I to do that? Can I make my way back to the drawbridge grate and run out again, the same way I came in? I expect the Flöbbertigôbbet will do everything in his power to prevent me from doing that." The tiny tiger eyeballed the windows. "Being a very fine and gracefully athletic Shorthair Classic Tabby, if I could get through the glass of a window, I could likely jump out and away from the building and possibly land outside the moat. The moat is deep for certain, and its waters would surely drown me if I fell in, but it's fairly narrow, and I might be able to soar over it if I kick out hard as I jump. Now—how am I to get through the glass?" Kitten looked at his various toys: all lightweight objects that would probably not even crack a window pane if tossed at it; though of course, Kitten had only paws, not hands, and couldn't possibly pick up and pitch objects about like a human. "Rats!" the feline snorted. "This is going to be difficult."

The cat's thoughts were interrupted by a loud knock at the door. Its crystal knob turned and the prince entered, a peculiar gleam in his eye.

Kitten turned and looked at his adversary. If the tabby had been capable of smiling, there would have been a Cheshire-cat grin lighting his handsome little face. The game was fully afoot now: he knew who was who and what was what, and the prince knew that he knew it. The masks were gone and the fight would begin, finally, though Kitten's first action wouldn't be a suicidal physical assault.

There was a powerful exhilaration racing through the tiny tiger's body. He was, after all, a full-blooded Classic Tabby: a feline made for the chase; bred to be, as a cat fancier might say, a "working cat" whose *raison d'être* was the hunt. Perhaps the object of this hunt was not the usual simple one: a mouse, for instance, who had been pilfering from the kitchen; no, the object of this chase was more abstract and complicated—the ultimate object was triumph over an imposing supernatural enemy.

The tip of Kitten's tail twitched as he regarded his quarry, and he snorted softly.

The Flöbbertigôbbet smiled.

The tabby considered his immediate options, and quickly chose the one he liked best. "I'll try a psychological approach to start out," he thought. "I won't say anything. I'll just look cool and calm and not say a bloody word, and that will give him nothing to feed on; nothing to manipulate or twist, no fuel for his conniving ways."

The Flöbbertigôbbet continued to smile; his eyes practically oozing with an exaggerated *faux* innocence which served no purpose other than to amuse the Mephistophelean creature.

Kitten met his enemy's gaze straight on, and began to purr. It felt good to vibrate in that soothing way, so he increased the volume. Tumbling down onto one side, he rolled over to lie on his back with his legs flopped limply out to the sides in the teasing position he used with people when he wanted to be really, really bad: offering up his soft white belly for supposed rubbing when it was his secret plan to use his wonderfully effective teeth and claws to shred whatever hand might be foolish enough to reach down into the furry, vibrating, allegedly pleasurable trap.

The Flöbbertigôbbet rolled his eyes back and pursed his lips. "I don't think so," the prince said softly, and turned on his heel. The door was closed behind him as he exited, and the tabby rolled over and headed for his bed, where he curled up and shook with quiet cat-laughter.

The sun rose up into a pink sky the next morning. Kitten blinked wearily; startled out of a fine dream by the warm rays that struck him as he lay sleeping. "Ah, I'm still here," he said; looking at the cold, congealed mass of fatty sausage that sat untouched on the silver plate before him.

Kitten went to the automatic litter box that sat in a corner. As the cat stepped into it, two glowing infrared sensors inside the tray winked: a pair of demonic eyes that told the box's mechanical scooper that a visitor had arrived. The tabby hissed for the fun of it; swiping at the scarlet lights with a casual paw. "For crying out loud; even the loo in this place is possessed," he remarked. Knowing the ways of self-cleaning feline toilets, the tiny tiger went ahead and relieved himself, then went back to his soft bed and began to make plans. "I believe I should station myself by the door and wait," he decided. "That's the best way to get out, especially since my visitors always knock before they enter, practically telling me that now is the time to make a run for it." He trotted to the door and crouched beside it; ready to spring forward should a maid enter with another plate of greasy sausage.

"I hope I won't run into any of those greys when I get out of here," he thought. "I didn't see any on the way up, but the Flöbbertigôbbet was most likely keeping them concealed while he was trying to convince me that he's a good guy. I wonder why he pretended to be nice? Why didn't he just have me killed? Must have been part of the corruption plan Wolf told me about; the way he either enlists animals or kills them. Well, then—I guess it's time for me to die, eh? Judging from the look I saw in his eyes last night, that will be the new plan. Well, fine; just let him try—I'm ready for anything."

The cat sat poised, nose held to the crack of the door, as he waited for whoever might come to give him his chance to flee. After what seemed like a very long time, he heard shoes scraping against the marble of the hallway floor. Tensing himself, he got ready to spring.

The crystal knob turned slowly and a stiff-bristled broom pushed through the opening door, sweeping the cat to one side as the Flöbbertigôbbet entered and quickly shut the door. "Did you really think I wouldn't know that you'd be waiting there?" the prince asked.

Kitten didn't answer, still adhering to his original plan of verbal silence.

The Dark One looked down at the cat. "You're utterly powerless, you know. There's no point in plotting and scheming. You can't get out, and you certainly can't win in a fight against me. Why do you even think about it?"

Kitten didn't believe the creature could really read his thoughts, and decided that the Flöbbertigôbbet was simply making a guess as to his inner processes. Sitting back on his haunches, the feline glared up at the man.

"Okay—so I deceived you about your friends." The prince put his hands into the pockets of his trousers as he looked down at the cat; an expression of earnest regret on his handsome face. "Can you blame me? I want you to stay here with me; I want you to be my friend."

The tabby sensed something all of a sudden—it was just a feeling, but a very strong one: the Flöbbertigôbbet was afraid of him; Kitten was quite sure of it. He didn't know how he knew, but he was absolutely and thoroughly certain that the prince feared him.

With this new information at hand, the feline decided to change his plan, and abandoned his silence. "You set the fire to make sure that Wolf would bring me here, didn't you?"

The prince glanced quickly to one side, then looked down at the tiny tiger. "I wouldn't go to so much trouble for a mere cat."

"Liar!" Kitten jumped up to stand on all fours. "You don't know how to handle me, do you?" The tabby had been suddenly engulfed by a warm fire of inner knowing. "When I first got here, you thought I was just another other-world animal and you let your agents and monsters use their normal techniques on me. But soon after I arrived, you realized that I'm not just a simple ordinary cat." The feline paused, not fully understanding what was racing through his mind: truths that were beyond full comprehension. "You can't have me killed! I am more dangerous to you dead than alive! When I leave this container of flesh, I'll become a foe who can overcome you. And even now, in this frail little body, I am capable of winning a fight against you. You haven't lost a face-to-face contest with an enemy in a long, long time, but the last time you met someone like me, you were defeated! It's the truth—admit it!"

The Flöbbertigôbbet's brown eyes suddenly began to turn a hideously ugly yellow. Turning on his heel, he bolted from the chamber, slamming the door shut behind him. Kitten could hear a strange hissing and whooshing as something flew down the corridor away from his room.

"Oh, my," the tabby said softly, "this is strange. I feel like I turned into someone else; no, no, that's not it. I feel like I turned into my true self; a real one-hundred-percent me. I feel like; oh, I don't know what I feel like. This is too, too strange. What is happening to me?"

CHAPTER SEVEN

A Small War

The feline had returned to his soft bed for a nap, needing a bit of sleep so he could recover from both the encounter with the Flöbbertigôbbet and the meeting with his mysterious new self. He was roused from his slumber by a clanging noise: a silver dish had been deposited on the floor before him by the elderly maid, who snatched the plate of sausage and fled through the door.

The tabby looked at the contents of the new plate: apparently the same protein pellets he had been eating in the wild. "Well, that's nice." Taking a few into his mouth, he chewed cautiously as his sensitive taste buds verified that the substance was indeed not someone who might have once been a friend. Charging ahead with gusto, the hungry cat filled his stomach.

After taking a few sips from his gold water dish, Kitten sat back to consider his situation. "It seems that I no longer need fear death at the hands of the Flöbbertigôbbet. Imprisonment, yes, but not death. Well—confinement is better than being a condemned cat, I suppose." The tabby nodded. "So, I am back to trying to figure out how to escape." He gazed at his water dish. "If I were built differently, I could pick that up and toss it at a window and that might break the glass. However, I am not built differently, so that thought is useless. I could, I suppose, jump up and fling myself at the glass; no, no—such an action would leave me gashed and badly sliced up if I did succeed in breaking a window pane, and my wounded personage would fall into the moat and be lost. I need an open window with a wide sill if I am to make a proper leap that will allow me to land intact on solid ground." Kitten sighed. "This is going to take some doing; yes, it will. I am getting out of here alive, one way or another! True; it seems from that fit of super-knowing which I just went through that I could do a better job of fighting the Flöbbertigôbbet if I weren't in this body anymore, but I'm not ready to die yet. Wolf would be upset, and so would Dove, and my Lady: no, that's not the way right now."

The cat considered his options. "There seems to be only one practical possibility for me here. Since the Flöbbertigôbbet is afraid to kill me, I can assault him without fear of deadly retribution as he's going out of my room through the open door, then maybe, while he's distracted by the pain of whatever minor wounds I can inflict on him, I can make a run for it."

Kitten stared up at the clear bright-blue sky that was visible through the windows. "I wonder why I'm changing. I wonder why, when I looked at the Flöbbertigôbbet, I knew what he was feeling. Nothing like that has ever happened to me before. It felt; it felt good, but it was so strange; as if I was being pushed forward by a huge wave of something that came from outside myself. It's funny: I know I'm the same physical size I was yesterday, but inside, I feel bigger, somehow." The little tiger shook his head. "This is really odd."

The tabby started to his feet—he had heard a haunting canine howl, which was surely Wolf. "Maybe if I jump up and look out the window, she'll see me, and know that I'm alive!" Crouching down, he made the leap and grabbed onto the window sill. Pulling his head up, he peeked over the edge and spotted the General at her station at the leading edge of the drawbridge; her head hung low with grief. "She can't see me," the cat moaned and, losing his grip, he fell from his precarious perch and collapsed onto the floor. "If only I could do that communication thing she does when she calls her troops from far away, then I could tell her I'm still alive. But I don't know how to do that!" Kitten lay in a limp heap, overcome with misery. He was trying so hard not to allow himself to feel distress over his dreadful situation, but it was impossible, and with his beloved friend so close outside, it was torture.

The tabby rose to his feet and began to pace. Back and forth over the slick hardwood floor in tramping stomps of mad cat anger he went; back and forth and back again marched the caged tiger whose sadness and frustration had turned to fury. His aggravated trot soon switched into a fast gallop round and round the perimeter of the big room. He ran till his breaths were ragged and weary, then suddenly, he stopped. Standing upright under a window, Kitten put his front paws against the wall and let out a throat-ripping cry louder than any he had emitted in his short life. As his lips closed in the finish, he heard a canine howl that seemed to be an answer. "She heard me!" the cat cried. "She heard me!"

The door opened and the Flöbbertigôbbet entered the room, slamming the wooden panel closed behind him. He didn't look quite so handsome as usual: there were lines round his eyes, and his finely tailored suit was rumpled and soiled. "Kitten!" he snapped, a marked volume of menace boiling in his voice.

The tabby turned, his back to the wall. "What?" he snarled.

"Crying to the wolf is a useless act. There's nothing the creature can do. She's called for reinforcements, but they are powerless to help you. Perhaps you and your friends don't realize that my drawbridge is in fine working condition. I can push an electronic button to raise it any time I like, and when I do, there will be no way for any of the General's beasts to touch my castle. I leave it down now," the prince laughed, "because I like to give Wolf false hopes: it's so much fun to dash them down at the very last moment!"

Kitten didn't betray his intended action with either a snarl or a growl. Unlike the General, he was free of the *Canis lupus* etiquette which dictates that a fighter must warn an enemy before attacking. Leaping forward and up with amazing power, the suddenly airborne feline flew onto the Flöbbertigôbbet's head and dug into its scalp with every one of his claws.

A hideous, nonhuman roar erupted from the prince. As his hands reached up to grab at the cat, the little tiger noted with considerable alarm that they were no longer the perfectly manicured appendages of a fine gentleman—rather, they were the horrible clutches of a savage beast: huge, rough, dark; equipped with long, sharp talons that could tear through the armored hide of a rhinoceros.

Kitten looked up in terror . . . the high domed ceiling of his grand room appeared to be falling down towards his head. But no; that wasn't what was happening—in reality, the prince was growing; shooting up to a height that would make dear grizzly bear look short in comparison.

The tabby leapt off the beast's head, doing an acrobatic rollover in the air before landing flat on all fours. Running to the farthest corner of the room, the cat cowered under a low table there and peeked out at his opponent.

The Flöbbertigôbbet smiled at Kitten with the horrible glee of a happily unnatural reptile. He stood a good twenty feet tall now; twenty feet of solid bulging muscle guarded by a heavy oil-slick-colored skin of spines and scales which could repel assault by the most ferocious of animals. The prince's custom-tailored wool suit, shredded by his rapid growth spurt, lay in sorry little piles about his ugly clawed feet.

The monster laughed; his voice deep and rough, emitting a dreadful scraping scratchiness that made Kitten's fur stand on end. "Would you care to try another assault?" the beast asked.

The tabby took a deep breath. Striding forward from his spot under the table, he went to the prince's feet and parked himself. Looking up at the towering fiend's head, he snorted in disgust. "Listen, you son-of-a-bitch!" he shouted. "You can surprise me, but you won't succeed in scaring me. You can't kill me, and I know it, so don't waste any more of my time on this fright-show nonsense." The little tiger moved a few steps closer to the door, ready to make a run for it. "I need another nap—I'd appreciate it if you'd leave me alone."

The Flöbbertigôbbet's eyes darted to the right, then to the left. He made an angry gurgling sound deep in his throat, and poof! the beast vanished in a puff of stinking yellow smoke.

Kitten sighed heavily. "So much for making for the open door." Going to his bed, he curled up and fell asleep.

•——•——•——•——•——•——•

The tabby woke with a start. The elderly maid had appeared, bearing a plate of pellets. "Hey!" Kitten greeted her as she set down the full dish and picked up the empty one. "How are you today, ma'am?"

"How am I?" The woman's tired green eyes peered carefully at the little feline. "How am I?" She tilted her white-haired head to one side.

"Yes, you—how are you?"

The maid blinked nervously. "No one ever asks me that."

"Why not?"

"They're all too busy, I expect. Everyone's always too busy." The woman straightened up as best she could: a difficult task for a lady with a pronounced dowager's hump. "I suppose I'm too busy, too; to be

168

talking to a cat." She groaned softly and let her posture go again, unable to make her ancient spine straight.

"Don't you like cats?"

"I've never met one before."

"Really?"

The tabby extended a paw. "I'm Kitten. And you are?"

The maid shook the offered paw gently. "Mary Collins."

"Nice to meet you, Mary."

"I'm pleased to make your acquaintance, Kitten."

"How long have you been working here, Mary?"

"Not too awfully long: a few months."

"Is it a good job?"

"It's all right. It keeps food on my table, and gives me a roof to sleep under."

"You live here, then?"

"No. I live beyond the wall, about two miles from here. This job pays my rent."

"What's it like beyond the wall?"

"Crowded, sir—crowded."

"Unpleasantly so?"

"Well . . . I didn't think much about how unpleasant home is until I started coming here. After all, I didn't know any different. But the first time I stepped past the wall, and there were no other people whatsoever, and no sound except a gentle wind: it was wonderful. I'd never heard quiet before."

"You'd never heard quiet before?" The little cat was amazed.

There was a sound out in the hallway; a muted shuffling. The maid turned away. "I have to go, sir."

"Goodbye, Mary."

"Bye."

Kitten considered the woman who had just left. He was not accustomed to meeting people with a look of quiet despair in their eyes. In his Lady's house, all had what they needed to enjoy lives of basic contentment. Things were good in the country shire; though life may not have been thoroughly perfect for the Lady and her circle of friends and employees, abject misery was something rarely encountered. The tabby had seen the look of unrelenting misery in Mary's eyes, and wondered about it.

"Well," the cat said to himself. "Perhaps, if I succeed in winning my fight against the Flöbbertigôbbet, the source of Mary's suffering might vanish. I don't know where her pain comes from, exactly, but since her basic needs are being met and she's clearly still miserable, the despair must have something to do with evil; it must be a thing for which her vile employer is ultimately responsible."

The tiny tiger began to eat as he considered his personal dilemma. "I must make some sort of plan," he thought, "a practical strategy must be devised. But this will be very difficult, considering that I've changed to the point where I'm suddenly unpredictable to myself. Now, the Flöbbertigôbbet—he's fairly predictable. He'll likely be coming here several times a day with the intention of tormenting me. I know he likes to make others suffer just for the fun of it; he showed that side of himself already. Yes, I'm quite certain he will be coming back to visit often, even though he's a bit afraid of me.

"But predicting my own behavior—that's another matter. I certainly didn't expect that I'd be reading the

Flöbbertigôbbet's nasty little mind, and I most definitely did not ever dream that I would be more dangerous to him dead than alive. Now, how can that be? How could a dead cat be a danger to a living immortal?" Kitten snorted. "Oops—I almost started to believe that nonsense about him being immortal. I have to remember not to do that. Oh, bloody hell!" The tabby groaned—the crystal doorknob was turning.

The Flöbbertigôbbet entered in solid door-slamming style, resplendent in a new suit of deep-grey wool pinstriped with barely perceptible streaks of a lighter charcoal. His face was once again smooth and unlined; his eyes youthful and innocent. "Looks like he had a face-lift," Kitten muttered. Rising to his feet, the cat addressed his visitor. "Nice threads!" the feline declared. "Made a trip to Savile Row, did you?"

The prince smiled sweetly.

Kitten waved at his plate with a front paw. "Would you care to join me for lunch?"

"No, thank you—I don't eat."

"That's what I've heard."

The prince smiled even more broadly; showing off his perfect, straight, dazzling-white teeth to their fullest glory.

"So, Mister Flöbbertigôbbet: why am I once again blessed with the absolutely unmatchable pleasure of your fine company?"

The prince put the fingertips of one hand to his mouth and giggled.

Kitten tensed up; his body turning into a tight knot of muscle. Surely it was not a good thing when the source of all evil giggled. But maybe it was just a ploy: an attempt at psychological warfare; an action designed to make the cat feel insecure. The tabby took a deep breath, then exhaled. "Perhaps it's time to go back to the silent approach," he decided. "Heck—I can be way more enigmatic than that guy." He sat back on his haunches and put his face into neutral: ears up but not unusually alert, mouth relaxed, eyes expressionless.

The Flöbbertigôbbet blinked his sparkling brown eyes as a look of exquisite happiness came onto his face. Putting both hands into his trouser pockets, he broke into a lively little jig-like tap dance.

Kitten was instantly annoyed by this. Such a display seemed highly inappropriate to the cat. For one thing, there was no music to be heard, and the tabby knew that dancing and music went together as an unassailable unit. To dance without music was certainly a sign of insanity, but even if there had been instrumental accompaniment, this expression of what seemed to be a form of celebration was certainly improper, considering the situation. The small tiger's tail-end started to twitch as his irritation began to grow more and more intense.

The prince's performance grew livelier and more ambitious. He began to tap harder and faster as he twirled in tight little circles; spinning about like an overly energetic girl competing for ribbons at a country fair.

Kitten began to get very angry indeed. "Wolf is out there worried to death about me and this idiot is doing a flipping dance," he thought. "She's probably not even eating; just sitting there staring at the grate as she waits for additional troops to arrive. She's out there suffering in terrible misery and that good-for-nothing monster is dancing away like it's a blooming May-Day celebration. Damn him!" The tabby sprang to his feet, crying out, "This is totally inappropriate!" He galloped forward and leapt onto the right leg of the Flöbbertigôbbet as the villain raised the limb high for a lively chorus-girl kick-out.

The cat was seized by two strong hands, pulled off the leg, and thrown into the air at high speed. Kitten saw the wall he was flying toward and realized he was heading for a serious injury. Not death; no, but frightful injury; yes, and great pain.

Closing his eyes, he hunched his body into a ball and pushed his back legs against the air. Now, we all know that one cannot push against the atmosphere, don't we? But Kitten was able to do this supposedly impossible thing. The air was suddenly his personal friend, and thickened itself into an elastic wall so the feline could use it as a trampoline. Bouncing off the gentle barrier of cooperative oxygen, he flew back into the general direction from which he had come and right into the face of the Flöbbertigôbbet.

The tabby fell to the floor as the prince howled in anger and surprise. A stream of very unpleasant obscenities flowed from the fiend's mouth as Kitten trotted about him in small circles, hoping to get a chance to bolt through the door when the opportunity presented itself. The cat looked up at his cursing opponent; a satisfied look on his face. "That kind of language will get you nowhere, sir," the little tiger cheerily remarked.

The prince's expression was very dark. "I'll be back," he snarled, "I'll be back!" Dashing past the feline with amazing speed, the Flöbbertigôbbet exited in a lightning blur; slamming the door so hard that one of its wooden panels cracked slightly.

Kitten took a few deep breaths, then headed for his bed. Lying down, he attempted to encourage himself. "I have to try very hard not to be upset about all this. I mean; I am enjoying small successes against that nasty fellow but, when all is said and done, I'm still trapped in this room. I must not give in to despair." He pondered the way the atmosphere had thickened for him. "If I could get the air to do that for me right now, I could perhaps form it into steps, climb up to a window, and sit on the air as if it were a wide sill, then Wolf could see me. Can I do that?" He put out a front paw and held it high. "Dear atmospheric friend!" the tabby commanded. "Make yourself into steps for me!" He rose and felt his way around; no magic staircase had been formed for him. "Oh, well," the cat mumbled. "I tried."

He went to his plate and took a few bites of pellets. "I must not give in to despair," he told himself as he chewed, "I must not give in to despair. Oh, no—not again!" The crystal doorknob was turning.

The enemy entered. He was carrying a cage.

Kitten started backwards. The cage was one of those awful cat carriers, just like the one that had been used to transport him when he was taken from his mother. The green plastic box had doors made from metal bars on its roof and at one end.

The Flöbbertigôbbet set the carrier down on the floor. "You need a different room," he stated grimly.

The tabby's black pupils grew very large. "I'd rather die than get in that box," he said.

"Your death will not be necessary," the prince replied.

"That's what it'll take to get me into that mobile prison!" the cat declared.

"I don't think so," the Flöbbertigôbbet responded, and took a step forward.

Kitten sprinted to the farthest corner of the room and huddled there in terror, and the prince followed. Just as he got within grabbing distance of the tabby, the feline took off at a gallop and escaped to the opposite corner of the big chamber. The routine was repeated several times, and soon it became clear that Kitten's panic was causing him to become predictable. The Flöbbertigôbbet, having figured out the tabby's pattern of evasion, charged at the feline, then feinted to one side; doubling back and flinging himself onto the tiny tiger's body as the cat shot forward in what he thought was a safe direction.

The prince's strong hands clutched the cat tightly. "I've got you now, little beast!"

Kitten snarled in fury as his enemy rose from the floor and carried the wriggling feline to the carrier. "You're not getting me in there!" the cat shouted.

"You have no choice!" the prince retorted.

"You wanna bet on that?" the tabby snapped.

The Flöbbertigôbbet pinned the diminutive kitten under one of his powerful arms as he opened the top door of the carrier. Grabbing the struggling, fighting cat with both hands again, he set him over the opening. "Down you go!" the prince cried, trying to push the squirming tiger into the hole.

Kitten was no idiot, however. Sticking all four legs out as far as they could go, he braced his feet against the edges of the hole; making himself slightly bigger than the opening. The prince pushed and pushed, but he could make no progress against the self-enlarging feline. "This is ridiculous," the frustrated fiend muttered. "It's only a tiny cat—how can it be stronger than me?" No matter how much he tried, he could not get Kitten's legs to give up their fight.

The tabby was as surprised as the prince. He had been sure that his efforts at evading imprisonment inside the cage would be nothing more than futile tokens of resistance, but here he was; a mere kitten small enough to be held in one hand of an average-sized human adult; successfully fighting off a physically strong man's attempt to overwhelm him. The feline was very surprised, and quite pleased.

The Flöbbertigôbbet, seeing his struggles were getting him nowhere, snorted in disgust and released the cat. Kitten ran to the corner nearest the door, where he sat back on his haunches, leaned his spine against the wall, and gazed at his opponent. The prince, crouching by the carrier, stared back at him with eyes that were dark in every sense of the word.

This silent exchange of looks went on for some time, then the Flöbbertigôbbet stood. Closing the top grid of the cage, he picked it up by its handle and carried it to the door. "Don't try to make a run for it," he said to the cat.

"Me, try to escape?" he asked innocently.

The door was slammed shut behind the exiting prince.

The tabby's black-furred tail end, poking out between the splayed hind legs of the upright-seated cat, quivered in an expression of feline tension. "I won that little battle," Kitten said to himself, "though I surely don't know how." He shook his head. "But I'm still inside a prison."

The captive looked up and stared at the bright sky visible through the windows. "If I'm not careful, I'll get truly depressed, and if that happens, then my mind will fail to work correctly, and I won't be able to find a solution to my dilemma."

He started, hearing the doorknob turn. The prince entered again. His face was nonthreatening, bearing no trace of malice or evil intent; not even a hint of devilish amusement was present in his visage. He walked to the cat and sat down on the floor before him. "Listen, little fellow," the Flöbbertigôbbet said earnestly. "Can't we come to some sort of agreement? It seems such a waste for a talented youngster like yourself to spend the rest of his life locked up in a room, doing nothing whatsoever when he could be achieving great things. We should come to terms of some sort, so you can be free, and make the most of your life."

"Terms? Like what? Are you going to offer me a gold-trimmed sports utility vehicle and throw in plastic surgery that will provide me with opposable thumbs so I can drive the damned thing?"

"I wouldn't insult a noble feline like yourself with such a tasteless offering. No, you need position and power, not toys. You should be a ruling prince, like me."

"With power over whom? I have no desire to rule my fellow animals."

"I was thinking of the humans."

"I certainly don't want to rule them!"

"Don't you realize how much you could do for your animal friends here if you were in charge of the humans?"

"Like what? What could I do for them?"

"You could put a stop to the bombs that are being designed."

"What bombs?"

"The ones that will wipe out all animal life while leaving plant life intact and the soil clean and fertile: the bombs which will allow the humans to move into the natural hemisphere."

Kitten stared at the prince. The cat's inner light had switched on again, and he could see into the heart of the beast before him. "You're lying, lying, lying! No bombs are being designed, and even if they were, you don't have enough power to put me in control of the human hemisphere. You are a big fat walking talking lie! You want me to bond with you, be your little chum, and lie happily in your arms as you stand in the front gate before the army out there so I'll be disgraced in front of Wolf and Bear and First Horse and Pony: animals who, unlike you, are true-blooded royalty. Your lies are so obvious and odious that they stink up this great big room with their foul stench. Get away from me!" The cat leapt to his feet and hissed with all he had.

The Flöbbertigôbbet stood and looked down at the tabby. "Very well. You have chosen your fate, then." Closing his eyes, he vanished in a puff of sulfurous smoke.

"That creature is an animated cliché," Kitten muttered, "and I believe I truly hate him; I really do. It's unfortunate that he seems to be succeeding in breaking me down. I think I just used up my very last bit of fight; my very last bit. I'm empty now." The feline let his head hang low as a deep sigh issued forth from his tired little body.

The cat's ears twitched back suddenly—a flopping-squishing noise was coming from the far end of the corridor; growing louder as it moved toward his door. The tiny tiger's nose detected a nauseating odor. "Oh, no," Kitten moaned. "It's the signature scent of the grey monsters."

The tabby, now devoid of all hope, didn't try to make a run for it, and stood quietly watching as the Flöbbertigôbbet entered the room with three very large greys behind him. The prince carried a sturdy wire-mesh cage big enough to admit a full-grown Labrador Retriever. Setting it down on the floor, Kitten's enemy opened its door and waited as his slimy servants went to the cat and arranged themselves in an inescapable semicircle before him.

A grey reached forward with one big, ugly hand and snatched the unresisting feline. It popped the little tiger into the cage, and the Flöbbertigôbbet closed the door and bolted it securely shut.

Kitten lay on his side in the portable prison as it was lifted by two of the monsters. The prince stepped out into the castle corridor, and the greys followed with their miserable burden.

The feline stared out at the passing environment; his eyes glassy and listless. The corridor walls that had worn exquisite carved-mahogany panelling a short time ago were no longer fine and beautiful; they were now seeping barriers of mildewed, rough stone. Kitten looked down through the metal-grid bottom of his cage: the lovely white-marble tiles that had graced the hallway floor were gone; replaced by a situation which resembled a long-abandoned sewer. The tabby closed his eyes, unwilling to observe any more of the castle's physical degradation.

After a few minutes of sloppy splashing about, the group came to a halt, and the cat opened his eyes again. The Flöbbertigôbbet, his fine calfskin shoes covered with muck, was standing before a low door of rusted iron. "Your new accommodations," the beast said with a smile. He pushed the heavy door open, and a black hole was revealed. "In you go!" the prince crowed. Removing the limp cat from his cage, he tossed the tiny tiger into the hole and slammed the door shut.

Kitten rolled over as he hit moist ground. "Ohhh," he moaned. "This is dreadful; absolutely dreadful." His prison cell reeked of odors too horrible for a sensitive feline nose to comfortably tolerate, and every surface was damp with unseeable filth. It was utterly black inside the small chamber, with not even the tiniest speck of light which a set of *Felis catus* night-vision eyes could grab onto and magnify.

The tabby felt his away about as best he could. The room, if one wanted to call it that, was very small; so compact that an adult human would not have been able to stand upright within it or lie down at full length. The low door, through whose frame a man would have had to crawl if he wished to enter, had a small opening with a hinged metal flap covering it that was presently locked shut from the outside. "Must be for meal delivery," Kitten decided. There were no water or food dishes in the chamber, and to make matters still worse for the meticulously clean cat, there was no litter box. "This is truly disgusting and horrible," the little feline muttered.

Resting his spine against a wall of damp stone, Kitten sat upright and thought about the filth that covered him. Picked up by a grey's slimy hand and then thrown onto the layer of putrescent matter that covered floor of his noxious prison—the tiny tiger was a bundle of matted, foul-smelling fur. He sniffed at a front paw, and recoiled in horror. "I can't possibly lick this disgusting stuff away; I simply cannot. I guess; I guess I'll just have to sit here and rot." A tear rolled down his dirty cheek. "Oh, no—I'm crying! Cats aren't supposed to cry! But; but what does it matter, anyway: what does it matter? Nothing matters anymore." Lacking the strength to weep properly, the feline slumped down on one side to lie in the moist filth of his dungeon.

It was hard to know how long the tabby had been lying there. It might have been days; it might have been weeks. Time was warped inside the awful black hole; perceptions were slanted and cockeyed, causing Kitten to lose all faith in his senses. His auditory abilities, for example; the feline heard noises now and then, but they were muffled, strange, and, having no visible source, were likely imagined. No doubt the speck of light which had just appeared before the despairing cat's half-shut eyes, hovering in the fœtid atmosphere of the room like a lost firefly: that was a hallucination brought on by the lack of decent food, clean water, and external stimuli.

Kitten giggled at the tiny dot of luminosity. "Oooh, hoo! I'm seeing things now. Little lights are coming to visit; here to keep me company in my hellish cell. Yes, indeed—I'm going crackers for sure." The feline watched in dazed fascination as the sparkle of gleaming white suddenly began to pulsate with an increasing brilliance. He blinked twice, and the speck flashed outward; exploding into a burst of illumination so powerful that it made the tabby cover his eyes for fear of being blinded.

Kitten rose to his feet and backed up against the wall. This wasn't a hallucination—this, the cat knew somehow, was an opening between two dimensions. The feline squinted into the pure brilliance before him, and a radiant figure stepped out of it and into the dungeon. As the visitor's feet touched the dank floor of the prison, the rift of light closed in a quick flash; vanishing behind the fabulous being it had just delivered.

Glowing with a self-produced illumination, a marvelous bird stood before the tabby. Quite like an eagle, it was even grander than those stately creatures, with feathers of shining iridescent purple and gleaming bright gold adorning its regal form. Its body emitted a fine perfume; waves of cinnamon and frankincense filling the chamber.

It fixed its pair of sparkling black eyes on the tiny tiger. "Kittenus Maximus!" The male bird's voice was very deep, and projected a sweet clarity unheard in normal worlds. Gazing at the unresponsive cat, he repeated his address: "Kittenus Maximus!"

The little tabby was confused. "Pardon?"

"Kittenus Maximus!"

The cat drew himself up to his fullest height. "Yes, sir?"

"Greetings, Kittenus Maximus. I am The Phoenix; The One. I've come to free you."

"Oh." Kitten dropped his gaze, feeling that he was not good enough to look directly into the eyes of his visitor. "Thank you, sir."

The phoenix did a quick visual examination of the cat. "You are covered in filth, Kittenus Maximus. With your kind permission, I will clean you."

The tabby bobbed his head. "Please do."

The visitor stepped forward; his golden taloned feet gliding unsullied through the foul muck of the dungeon floor. "Don't be afraid—this will not harm you." Standing before the pitiful feline, the great bird opened his mouth and sent out a fire of brilliant purple and green. Engulfing the cat, the cool flames consumed the soil that covered him without burning his skin or fur; leaving his coat clean and soft again.

The phoenix stepped back. "You did well, Kittenus Maximus. Not all were certain that you would make it this far, but I knew you could do it."

"'All'? Who is 'all'? And who are you?" The tabby continued to look downwards; intimidated by the extraordinary purity he had perceived in the bright flashing eyes of the bird. "You are not the Flöbbertigôbbet in disguise; of that much I am certain."

"You are quite correct about that, Kittenus Maximus! I am, well; one could say I am the opposite of the Flöbbertigôbbet, and even a bit more than that."

"I . . . I could see that, somehow, in, uh; your eyes. But why do you address me by that strange title?"

"Because it is yours. It has been waiting for the day when you earned the right to be called by it. I find it a very great pleasure indeed; being able to finally address you by that name."

"Oh." Kitten squirmed. "I don't understand," he sighed.

"It's been a while since you've had fresh water. Would you like a drink?"

The tabby nodded. "Yes, please; sir phoenix—I would like that very much."

The bird spread his huge pair of light-flashing wings out as far as they could go within the tight confines of the walls and bowed his purple head down low towards the floor of the dungeon. He blew out a gentle breath onto the mucky surface, and a tongue of rich yellow flame appeared; instantly forming itself into a bowl of brightest gold filled with crystal-clear water. The phoenix lifted his head. "Drink!"

The tabby went to the gleaming dish and drank. It was the sweetest water the feline had ever tasted; a vital liquid that jumped into his mouth and down his throat to tickle the inside of his gullet and stomach with effervescent energy. Kitten emptied the bowl, then looked up; keeping his eyes fixed on the phoenix's purple chest. "That's the best water I've ever had! I'm not even hungry anymore!"

"Yes." The bird nodded. "That's quite a bit better than what the Flöbbertigôbbet has been giving you."

Kitten became nervous; thinking of his enemy. "Do you suppose he's hovering about outside my door?"

"No, no—he's gone."

"Gone? Are you sure?"

"Absolutely. He cannot tolerate my presence. He would have fled the immediate vicinity as soon as I stepped through the rift and into this cell. He would not be able to stay in the fortress with me here."

"You have such power over him? Who are you?"

The phoenix's eyes twinkled merrily. "Now, if I tell you that, there will be no more mysteries to keep you entertained. What is life without mysteries?"

"For me, it would be a flat and boring existence indeed; a mere waiting for death to come."

"The water did its work—you are yourself again."

"Perhaps you can tell me about something. I have a feeling, from looking at you, that you know a great many things. I have a question."

"Yes?"

"When I came to the fortress and started getting into fights with the Flöbbertigôbbet, some very unusual things started happening to me. I read the prince's mind a couple of times, and I pushed against the air like it was solid, and, uh; these little kitten legs of mine were so strong that the Flöbbertigôbbet couldn't force me into the small cage and had to go for a bigger one. An adult cat has strong enough legs to keep itself out

185

of a cage, but I'm only a kitten. Strange things have been happening!"

"Yes; it would seem that way to you."

"What was going on? Cats just aren't supposed to do things like that!"

"It wasn't entirely a matter of a cat doing it. It was also my agents helping you fight."

"Ah—you have agents, too."

"There is a very large war going on, Kittenus Maximus. The Flöbbertigôbbet and your General aren't the only ones with armies."

"So your agents—the ones who helped me—were; they're invisible?"

"I am not of this . . . shall we say, universe? At least not anymore, so my ways are a bit different."

"And you are going to get me out of here?"

"Yes."

"Won't that be awfully difficult?"

"My arrival here was difficult. Certain situations had to be just right in order to allow a physical opening into this universe to become a reality. But now that I am here; no, getting you out of this cell won't be difficult at all."

"What about this new name of mine?"

"You are full of questions, Kittenus Maximus."

"Cats are known for their curiosity."

"Yes, they are."

"So why has this name been waiting for me to earn it?" Kitten finally overcame his insecurity, and looked the phoenix straight in the eye. It felt odd doing that; the cat had a strange feeling that if he did it for too long, his heart would explode from an overdose of power. He decided to drop his gaze once more to the bird's safer chest. "What's the game, sir?"

"The game? You are destined to fight manifestations of the Flöbbertigôbbet, young fellow, both in this world and in your own."

"Destined to fight, eh? Am I destined to win?"

"It is time to go, Kittenus Maximus." The phoenix raised a glittering wing, and the iron door of the cell swung open.

Knowing the question about his destiny would not be answered, the tabby stepped out into the dim light of the stone-walled passageway. He turned to face the phoenix, who was behind him. "The greys: what about the greys?"

"I have put them to sleep. They will not awaken until I allow it."

"I see." Kitten looked at the muck through which he would have to proceed. "I'm going to get all dirty again."

"No, you won't. The filth will slide right off of you, in the same manner in which it fails to adhere to me. Now go ahead, young soldier."

"Which way?"

"To your left. The exit is not far off." The One walked behind the cat as they began to make their way along the passage. The bird had increased in size as he emerged from Kitten's cell, and the broad shoulders of his body almost filled the width of the corridor.

The feline looked down at his front feet as he walked through the sloppy muck of the passage, observing with interest the manner in which the slime formed into neat globs that slid right off his paws without leaving a trace on his fur. "Are my friends still out there?" the tabby asked.

"Yes. Wolf will not give up a siege once she has begun it. Besides, her love for you is so great that there is no force in the world which could cause her to abandon the hope that you will come out alive. You have become like a son to her."

"She's like a mother to me. I wish I hadn't doubted her. I should have known she wouldn't leave me."

"You're very young, Kittenus Maximus. The errors of youth are easily forgiven, if only you will forgive yourself. You think of that particular mistake more often than you should."

"Yes, I do," Kitten agreed. "Do you know; did the Flöbbertigôbbet ever get around to raising the drawbridge?"

"Yes. The General's reinforcements arrived not long ago, and when the prince saw the rhinos and elephants, he raised the ramp. Lowering it and opening the grate will be a simple matter for you, and once you've done that, Wolf's army will come inside and lay waste to the building; something they've been unable to do before but will succeed at today. Destruction of the castle will be a significant achievement; excellent for the morale of the troops and an effective way of slowing down the beast's progress. It won't be easy for him to build a new stronghold—it will require much hard physical work, as his magic is limited to brief bursts which are often impressive but almost always short-lived. He can't just snap his fingers and create a new castle."

"His magic may be limited, but he is quite powerful. Everyone says he's immortal, and can't be defeated."

"But you never accepted that, did you?"

"Nope." The pair left the passageway and entered the central courtyard, and the feline looked to his right. "There's the exit!" The tabby sprinted over the bare dead earth that had replaced the elegant flagstone pavement; the latter having been yet another temporary magical illusion.

Running to the iron grate, Kitten looked at the solid wood barrier that was closed against its outer side. "I can open that, you say?"

"Yes. Here—climb up onto my shoulder, and you'll be able to reach that red button at the side of the grate. Push it twice, and the drawbridge will drop as the grate is pulled up into its open position."

Kitten did as he was told; getting onto the bird's shoulder by way of his outstretched right wing, which was held down to the earth so the tabby could climb up its length. The feline reached high with his paw and pushed the small button twice, then fell to the ground. "What; where did he go?" The phoenix had disappeared.

CHAPTER EIGHT

Rhinos Rule!

The recumbent wolf raised her head. "Attention!" she cried. "Drawbridge coming down! All stand ready!" The canid jumped to her feet and stood at the open edge of the moat, prepared to fight whatever might be coming out across the slowly lowering ramp, as the army in back of her put itself into battle stance. A troop of over one hundred white rhinoceroses assembled in front, with a company of nearly two hundred elephants waiting behind the horned chargers' armored rear ends. The original battalion of war-horses stood poised and ready to follow in the elephants' wake; their number now fortified by the presence of jackals, bulls, wolves, lions, tigers, panthers, ocelots, lynxes, eagles, falcons, boa constrictors, pythons, grizzlies: countless fight-ready animals had come from all over the natural hemisphere.

"Wait for the command!" the General shouted. First Horse, standing in the forefront beside the grouping of rhinos, repeated the order in her far-reaching voice.

The drawbridge was very slow to come down; the heavy wooden structure lowering inch by inch as the iron grate reluctantly squeaked its way upwards. Wolf was about to explode with tension, seeing nothing at all in the gate's opening as the ramp gradually revealed more and more of the fortification's courtyard entrance. When finally the leading edge of the bridge reached the canid's nose, she looked over it to see the little cat sitting on the metal threshold; a look of confusion on his young face.

"Wait!" the General cried. She leapt up onto the still slightly raised edge of the lowering drawbridge and, in a lightning flash, raced across the ramp to the open entrance, grabbed the tiny tiger with her jaws, and ran back to the outer wall. Setting Kitten safely down on the earth near the entry to the now-level drawbridge, the wolf raised her head and shouted, "Charge!" First Horse let out a deafening whinny and reared straight up, head tossing and forelegs pumping with excitement, and the attack was on.

Noses down as they headed for the bridge, the rhinos did what rhinos do best; mercilessly thrashing helpless earth into a shaking reverberating mass that cried out in testament to the incredible strength and power of the company of *Cerathotherium* who exploded into thundering forward motion with a swiftness of foot that was absolutely terrifying when paired with the white rhinos' massive weight and tremendous size. Kitten, frightened half out of his wits, clamped his eyes tightly shut and huddled as close to the moat wall as he could get, trying to squeeze himself into a shallow crack between two stones. "It's all right!" Wolf shouted into the tabby's ear. "We're safe—they won't step on you!"

"Are you certain of that?" the feline yelled. It felt to him as though the world was ending; the pounding was so very, very loud: unlike anything he had ever heard. How could the planet hold together under all that percussive force? Surely not even the sky itself would be able to withstand the thunder of more than one hundred galloping white rhinos, each and every one of their tank-like bodies over fifteen feet long and surpassing a hard-body weight of between four and five tons apiece; the destructive horde followed by a battalion of two hundred elephants even bigger than the chargers who preceded them; those trunk-nosed warriors stampeding in trumpeting fury before a mass of over half a million pounds of organized military horseflesh—how could anything endure all that power? And amongst the heavyweight might were creatures blessed with strengths of a different sort: lions who could leap onto a big grey and turn the vile monster into a collection of finely shredded canapés in nothing flat; slithering thirty-foot pythons who could spiral round and squeeze one of the prince's soldiers till the beast was face-to-face with Death itself and then swallow the slimy villain whole, rendering its body into a sweet slow mass of *pâté de* Thing with efficient reptilian stomach fluids; eagles who could land upon and rip open the semi-soft skull of a grey: yes, there were many excellent fighters on hand.

The tabby continued his attempts to make himself smaller as the army narrowed into a column and poured over the drawbridge. It was fortunate that the prince was a stickler for strong construction and first-rate engineering: his wooden ramp, though groaning slightly, bore well and soundly the countless tons of animal bodies charging over it.

Kitten slowly opened one eye, then the other, and watched as flying feet and hooves went raging past in a blur. After a few long moments, the heaviest troops had entered the fortress and the lighter-weight big cats, snakes, and others began to make their way inside. "Aren't you going with them?" he asked the General.

"They don't really need me right now," Wolf replied. "If the Flöbbertigôbbet was in there, it would be different."

"How did you know he's gone?"

"I could feel his absence. I don't know why he left or where he ran to—I just know he's not here." Wolf looked at the kitten. She was so happy to see him alive and still himself. The canid struggled to retain her dignity as her out-of-control tail thumped the ground with joy. "How did you manage to survive in there for so long?"

"How long has it been?"

"I didn't count the days as they went by; keeping track would have made me get too upset. But it has been quite a while since you went through that grate."

"I'm sorry I did that, ma'am—I'm sorry I went inside. I upset you, and I didn't; I didn't conquer the Flöbbertigôbbet."

"You came out alive and uncorrupted! No one has done that before. You have much to be proud of!" The General glanced up at the castle—one of the outer walls was starting to crack. "Come, son—let's back off a bit. They'll be filling in the moat with debris fairly soon, and I don't want you to be hit by flying stones."

They walked a safe distance away from the moat barrier and settled down in the grass. Kitten looked up at his reclining friend. "I didn't make it out of there on my own. Someone helped me, and brought me to the front entrance."

"Who?"

"A very large bird: a phoenix."

Wolf's eyes opened wide. "The phoenix?"

"I don't know if it was 'the' phoenix—it was a phoenix. My Lady has a painting in her house that shows a phoenix, and I overheard her explaining the meaning of the picture to one of her friends. I recognized it from that. I guess there must be a few of those birds about."

"There is supposed to be only one."

"Oh—that's why he said he was 'The One.' He did describe himself as 'the' phoenix, now that I think about it."

"This is most extraordinary," the General bobbed her head, "most extraordinary! It's been thousands of years since the phoenix was seen. In fact, it's been so long that most of us had come to believe that he was only a myth: a legend symbolic of things lost; forgotten in the distant past. I don't recall exactly what his complete story was, I'm afraid. I just remember only one phoenix could live at a single point in time, it was always male, it reproduced itself after a lifetime of several millennia, and; oh, my—how did that go?" Wolf watched as a slender turreted tower snapped in half and fell into the moat; its crashing accompanied by the joyous trumpeting of elephants. "Let's see—he was born, or regenerated, out of fire, somehow. I simply cannot remember the entire story."

"Well, I may not know his story, but I do know he isn't normal."

"Please—describe him!"

"He was the most beautiful thing I've ever seen. He appeared out of nowhere in my dungeon room. The Flöbbertigôbbet had put me into a horrible, filthy, dark cell after I refused to play his game the way he wanted me to."

"You're such a good cat! I knew he wouldn't be able to corrupt you."

"Thank you, ma'am. Anyway, I had been in the cell for a while; long enough that the total darkness and solitude were making me lose the balance in my mind, so to speak. I was lying there and a speck of light appeared before my eyes. At first I thought I was hallucinating, but then the light flashed so bright that I knew it was something real. In fact, somehow, I knew it was an opening into another place; a different universe or dimension. It felt, well; I really can't describe the feeling. I just knew what I knew, you know?"

"Yes, I know. Go on."

Kitten glanced at the castle—another tower had crashed into the moat. "The phoenix stepped out of the light into my cell. He was gorgeous! Looked quite a bit like an eagle, but he later showed that he was much bigger than that sort of bird. His feathers were fabulous purple and gold, and he glowed and had bright sparkling eyes that; at first, when I tried to look in them, I couldn't because I knew I was looking at someone who was so much better than me: better than anyone I'd ever met. He wasn't like me, or even like you. When he told me he was from another universe, it didn't surprise me at all; that's for certain."

"So he isn't the phoenix who was once said to dwell here?"

"He said he wasn't from this universe anymore."

"Ah—he might have been our phoenix, then, at one time."

"I guess so." The tabby nodded. "He had very impressive powers—he told me the Flöbbertigôbbet had left the fortress because he can't tolerate the presence of the phoenix, so he took off as soon as The One arrived."

"Sounds like a good bird to have as a friend."

"You say right, ma'am. He waved at the locked door of my cell and it opened. We walked to the gate without intervention from the greys—The One had put them all to sleep. He said he had agents helping me out earlier while I was having some fights with the Flöbbertigôbbet; fights that I won when it seemed to me that I shouldn't have been able to. The phoenix said his agents had helped me. They're invisible."

"Ah."

"He said he's the opposite of the Flöbbertigôbbet, and a bit more than that, too."

"Oh, my."

"And he kept calling me 'Kittenus Maximus.' He said it's my name." Kitten paused to watch a castle wall collapse into a heap of dust and rubble. "Said I had earned it." The tabby rubbed the side of his head with a forepaw to dispel a momentary itch. "He said I am destined to fight the Flöbbertigôbbet in both this world and my own."

"Are you destined to win?"

The little tiger's tail-end twitched. "That's exactly what I asked. The One was not eager to answer the question, so I didn't press him."

The wolf regarded the tabby carefully. "'Kittenus Maximus,' eh? Do you want me to call you that?"

"Doesn't seem fitting, ma'am. I'm just a cat, not a bloody Roman dictator."

"The name has a fine ring to it."

"Do you think it really is my true name, somehow?"

"If a bird stepped out of a flash of light, scared off the Flöbbertigôbbet, put greys to sleep, and freed me from a locked prison cell without even touching the door; I would tend to take his words seriously, son."

"Yes. Well, he didn't say I had to use the name. I'll wait until I'm older, I think, or until I've achieved something that makes me feel worthy of the appellation."

"You've already accomplished a great thing, Kitten: you came out of that fortress alive and uncorrupted. I don't believe that the assistance given to you by the phoenix detracts from such a singular achievement. Perhaps the fact that he aided you in your efforts, well; he's never helped anyone else escape from that horrible place." Wolf cocked her head to one side as she gazed down at the tabby. "When you first arrived here, I looked at you and thought, 'That little cat is special.' I didn't know in what manner or why. I just knew you were, and are, different."

"Oh—I almost forgot!"

"What?"

"The Flöbbertigôbbet can't kill me!"

"Pardon?"

"I was; I became like you while I was in the fortress. I couldn't communicate with other animals in precisely the same manner as you, but I received information in that way, and I read the Flöbbertigôbbet's mind. He's afraid of me, not the way he fears the phoenix, of course, but he doesn't know exactly how to handle me.

198

One reason he's afraid is because he knows that when I die—when I'm finished with this body—I'm going to become something more powerful than I am now: something capable of posing a serious threat to his continued existence. That's why he didn't kill me when I was in there. He planned to keep me alive in that awful little cell for as long as possible so he could delay the day when I'd make the change."

"I see. You don't plan to, well; die somehow, so you'll have a better chance of overcoming the Flöbbertigôbbet, I hope."

"No, no—it's not time for that yet. My death will come when it's supposed to, I guess, and not before. Anyway, I'd love to see how much trouble I can give that awful lying beast while I'm still in this body. Maybe fighting him will be too easy when I'm something else, eh? I'd like to see if I can beat him while I'm still just a little tabby cat."

The General's tail thumped the ground. "Thank you, son. I would miss you terribly if you abandoned your present form."

"Thank you, ma'am." Kitten licked Wolf's jaw with gentle affection.

As a result of the dedicated work of the rhinos and elephants, all the towers of the castle had been felled and most of the walls were down; the few upright sections which remained now being broken up by the vigorous double-horned assault of several of the armored creatures. Scores of grizzlies stood amidst the rubble, tossing pieces of masonry into the moat. War-horses were at the bears' sides, using their strong front legs to push big chunks of debris into the protective water-filled canyon that surrounded what had once been an impenetrable fortress. As the tabby looked at the ruin, he suddenly thought of his friend Dove. "I was in there for days, you said."

"Yes, it was quite a long while."

"My friend at home—she said she'd come here looking for me if I didn't return within a reasonable amount of time."

"Which friend is that?"

"A turtle dove. She showed me where the Door to this world is."

"Oh, yes—you've mentioned her before."

"She'll be worried about me."

"Yes, I expect she will."

"What if she comes after me? Dove is used to being outdoors, but she's never seen a grey before, and she doesn't know about the Flöbbertigôbbet's agents. The bird might come to serious harm if she comes looking for me. And if she brings any of her friends with her, they might be killed or captured."

"That is possible."

"I hope she hasn't come here already." Kitten began to pace back and forth in front of the wolf. "Oh, dear; oh, dear." He stopped and looked at the General. "Can you call out to your animals to find out if anyone's seen an other-world turtle dove?"

"I shall try." Wolf closed her eyes and sat quiet for several long moments; breathing hard from the difficulty of this rather detailed and far-ranging mental effort. Opening her eyes again, she looked at the tabby. "I can find no one who has seen her, but that doesn't mean she isn't here. It only means that no one has encountered a turtle dove known to be a foreigner."

Kitten began to pace again. "Oh, dear; oh, dear."

"You must go home to check on her, little friend. You will worry yourself to death if you do not."

"Yes, I believe you're right. Lady will be concerned about me, too. She must think I got out through a window and ran away. She'll be heartbroken—I'm her only child, so to speak. I need to go home; for a little while, at least."

"I will take you back to the emerald grove. How you're going to get to the Door itself, I don't know; but I can at least return you to the grove."

"What do you mean?" The tabby's eyes were huge with alarm. "You don't know where the Door is?"

"No, I don't. Do you remember seeing it in the emerald grove when you were there?"

Kitten's heart sank with a mighty thud, and his stomach began to ache. "No—it wasn't there. I came through the Door, then I went through the awful nothing place, and then the emerald grove appeared. Do I have to go through the terrible nothingness again? How would I get there? Oh, no; this is dreadful."

"Let's take it one step at a time, son. We'll get you back to the grove and see how things go. A solution may present itself when we get there."

The tabby's head drooped. "Yes, ma'am."

Wolf looked down at her tiny friend. "You are apparently a very important feline, Kittenus Maximus. In order to protect you from kidnapping attempts by the greys, we should take a substantial guard party with us: Bear, First Horse, maybe one or two rhinos, and a big cat. Would you like to ride Pony again?"

"Yes, please; ma'am."

"Wait here." The General trotted into the rubble of the ruined castle and emerged a few minutes later with the guard party: Bear, First Horse, two rhinos, and a male lion. The Haflinger trailed a bit behind them, breaking into a happy leg-kicking gallop as he spotted Kitten.

Racing up to the tabby, the equine dug his back hooves into the turf and slid to a stop. "It's a grand day, isn't it?" The pony whinnied with joy; his long platinum-blonde mane flying as he tossed his champagne-colored head in celebration. "The fortress is dust!"

"Like the dust of Babylon," Kitten replied.

"What's Babylon?"

"It's an ancient ruined city in my world. It's thousands and thousands of years old—I don't know how many thousands. It was one of the original seats of human civilization, with great libraries." The tabby paused. "I have to learn to read someday."

"Read? Why? What would you read?"

"History books. Where I'm from, animals and people live together. I spend a lot of time in a room filled with books—a library. There's all kinds of knowledge there."

"I see."

"I'll bet I could turn the pages of the books with my tongue," Kitten said.

"Yes, you could," Pony agreed.

Wolf had been talking with the regal-looking lion who stood between the pair of massive rhinos. Turning her head, the canid looked toward the east. It was afternoon now, with perhaps three hours of sunlight left. The time indicated by the position of the sun was of little concern to the animals, however, since all could navigate as easily at night as they could in midday. The General spoke again to the lion, then called to Kitten and Pony. "Let's go, boys! Dinner will be waiting for us in the spot where Jean-Baptiste left it."

"What about the army?" Kitten asked.

"They'll follow when they've finished their work here. The leveling of the building and filling in of the moat are not yet fully completed."

Pony knelt down on his forelegs. Kitten climbed up onto the equine's back, and the group entered the forest. Wolf and the big cat were in the lead with First Horse and Bear directly behind them, just ahead of the Haflinger, who was followed by the pair of white rhinos; one male and the other female. Kitten turned to look at the flesh-and-blood war tanks who trailed his mount; amazed by their extraordinary size. "They must surely be the biggest living things in this or any world!" the feline said to Pony.

"You're forgetting the elephants," the equine said, "and our whales, who are even larger still."

"Oh! You have an ocean, then!"

"Yes. It lies in the middle of our hemisphere, running from north to south."

"Does it divide your world so that animals can't travel from one border of the natural hemisphere to the opposite one?"

"It's not a total division—there are land bridges here and there which make crossings fairly easy when the tides are low."

Kitten craned his neck, trying to see the thick-maned lion who trotted in the front beside Wolf.

"That's one of my relatives!" the feline whispered to his mount.

"You must be very proud," Pony said.

"In my world, lions are some of the best hunters on earth."

"I suppose such a talent is useful when one is stuck on a barbaric planet!" the sharp-eared *Panthera leo* shouted.

Kitten, shocked by the comment, lost his balance and stumbled; his front paws scrabbling against the equine's spine. Pony came to an abrupt halt to allow the cat to regain a stable position, and one of the exceedingly heavy white rhinos, unable to stop in time, rear-ended the Haflinger with his double-horned snout. "Ow!" Pony cried, tumbling forward to his knees. The tabby fell onto the ground and rolled several times.

The company stopped, and the lion walked to the tiny tiger who lay in the grass, blinking his eyes rapidly in distress. "I'm sorry, son," the big cat said gently. "I expect you didn't intend to insult me."

"No, I didn't, sir. In my mind, such a statement is a compliment. I apologize—I didn't mean to accuse you of being a killer."

"It's all right. Even some here still overvalue a hunter's talent. Animals who don't have the ability sometimes attach a glamor to it; trying to make it seem like a wonderful thing. If they were me, and had my strength and reflexes and had to use them to do hideous things like slaying greys, they might understand why I would rather be almost anything except a soldier."

"I understand, sir."

"Let me restore you to the position I shattered with my rude retort." The big cat picked Kitten up in his mouth and deposited the tiny feline atop the Haflinger's spine.

"Thank you, sir."

"My pleasure, son." The lion strode off and rejoined Wolf at the head of the pack.

The company passed quickly through the narrow stretch of green forest and entered the burned area. Kitten groaned in pain; seeing once again the charred landscape where nothing lived. Even the bleak sands of the Sahara would have been preferable to this burnt desolation. A desert, at least, was natural, and would likely have had clean air. This place, however—the atmosphere, while no longer smoke-filled, still reeked of petroleum, and the crunchy charcoal underfoot was not natural terrain but a far-reaching testament to the Flöbbertigôbbet's destructive ways.

"Four days to get through this hellhole," Kitten muttered, glaring at a blackened tree stump; "four days."

A cloud of charcoal dust suddenly rose up from behind a low hill on the group's left. A dented SUV, white-painted and gold-trimmed under its layer of soot, came charging over the rise; veering crazily from one demented non-direction to another. Kitten wondered if the driver had been drinking. "Greys probably do get drunk," he thought.

"Halt," the canid said to her guards; apparently not too worried by the appearance of the vehicle, which carried a quartet of the usual monsters. "Come on, fools!" she shouted at the careening automobile. "Let's see you take on my rhinos!"

The machine came to a screeching, crooked stop a stone's throw away from the troop of animals. Lion leaned over and whispered in the canid's ear, "Please don't lose your temper, ma'am."

"I'm not angry," the General replied, "just thoroughly disgusted and, at the same time, strangely amused."

"I see."

The animals waited as the SUV's engine roared in neutral, then died down into quiet idle. Regurgitating laughter could be heard coming from inside the vehicle.

"Have at them, if you like," Wolf said to the rhinos.

"Our pleasure, ma'am!" the pair responded in unison. Lowering well-armed heads, the rhinos charged at the SUV; swiftly moving feet propelling them into a straight-ahead pounding line of sheer aggression. Screaming gears could be heard spinning and grinding into one another as the dim-witted driver, realizing the mistake he had made, attempted to get out of neutral and make a run for it. The rhinos could move far faster than this fool could shift, however, and in a short second their horns had made contact with the target. The vehicle was tossed onto one side; its vulnerable underbelly exposed.

The female rhino looked over the array of visible parts and selected the front axle as her victim. Dropping her head, she exploded into a short but effective charge; putting over eight thousand pounds of solid body weight behind her stout five-foot-long front horn as she rendered the SUV's front suspension useless. Her task finished with one mighty blow, the triumphant animal backed away from the crashed mess of mangled steel; a highly satisfied sashaying movement clearly visible in her Herculean hindquarters.

A moist gibbering emanated from the deranged chorus cowering within the disabled machine. "Come, ladies and gentlemen," Wolf said. "Let us leave the idiots to their own devices."

The group of animals trotted forward, leaving the crazed noises of the greys behind. "Those rhinos are terrific!" Kitten whispered to the Haflinger.

"Yes, they are marvelous. Don't talk much, and can't see terribly well, but they can put machinery out of action with tremendous effectiveness."

"Let's pick up the pace!" Wolf shouted. She broke into a slow, steady lope; and the company followed suit.

Kitten dug his front claws into a thick clump of blonde pony mane and attempted to let his standing body flex in harmony with the Haflinger's movement. "This is going to be a tough ride," the little feline muttered. "Cats ain't born to be equestrians!" Gritting his teeth, he proceeded to hang on as best he could; mentally preparing himself for hours of hard physical work—a suffering preferable to the indignity of asking Bear to once again carry him like a baby.

Wolf slowed to a leisurely walk as the company came over the top of a ridge. "Water and pellets just ahead!" she called out.

The tabby breathed a sigh of relief. "Time to rest!" he purred. Peering round the side of the Haflinger's sturdy neck, the tiny tiger could see a loose-knit band of wild creatures at the water containers: three heavy black draft horses, two elephants, a spattered-coat red-and-white long-horned bull, four wolves equal in size to the General, and a grizzly. A pair of golden eagles were parked on opposite ends of the great bull's lengthy horns; there being no trees or bushes in the area which the birds could use as perches. "What do you suppose all those animals are doing in this awful wasteland?" Kitten asked his mount.

"When the General called for reinforcements, she asked for a guard party to protect the water so the greys wouldn't spill or foul it," Pony replied.

The troop came to a halt at the first water container, and Kitten jumped down onto the ground. Leaping atop the inflated wall of bright-pink rubber, his claws carefully retracted, the feline lowered his head and drank his fill as Wolf addressed the band who had been standing guard over the drinking supply. When she finished telling them of the destruction of the stronghold, a cheer of exultation went up. The General waited until the shouts of joy died down, then said, "As one might expect, the Flöbbertigôbbet was not destroyed. He left the castle, that is true; but he's still around here someplace."

"One would not dare to dream otherwise, ma'am," the bull said. "If we hoped for more, we would surely be disappointed."

"Yes," Wolf replied.

"What is your next plan?" asked one of the eagles.

"At the moment, my main concern is to get this kitten back to his homeland. He has friends to report to in the other world."

"Oh—an other-worlder! How is he going to get back?" the eagle inquired.

The General looked at Kitten, who was busy filling his stomach; crouched down at a sack of carnivore pellets. "I'll take him to the emerald grove. How he is going to return to his particular Door from there, I really don't know."

"I see."

"We must make the effort and at least give him the opportunity to try, correct?"

"Of course, ma'am."

"The bulk of the army stayed behind to make certain the castle's thoroughly leveled and the moat filled in. Can you continue to guard the supplies here until the troops have come through again?"

"Yes, ma'am," the elephant said. "We'll stay."

"Thank you." Wolf went to a pool and began to drink.

Kitten, tummy well filled and thirst satisfied, sat down on the ground, leaned back against the wall of a wading pool, and let his body go limp in utter relaxation. Purring loudly, he looked over the landscape. The blackened ground—yes, it was certainly ugly, but the sky was quite pleasant to gaze upon. The sun had just set, and a sweet purple-red twilight was glowing from the horizon.

One of the bull elephants decided to enjoy a good back-scratching roll and lowered himself carefully down onto the ground. His stout legs waving in the air, he twisted and squirmed atop the crunchy black earth until his itching need was satiated. With a mighty grunt, he rolled back onto his stomach and rose to his feet.

As he settled into a secure stance, the elephant's long trunk lifted suddenly in alarm and began to poke at the air, searching for the scent of a perceived danger. His ears swung forward and open, their flaps extended to allow the great beast to catch the slightest of sounds.

Kitten's tiny ears perked up as he tried to hear what the elephant was listening to. After a bit of concentration, the feline detected a faint noise that reminded him of a household furnace: a soft, steady breath that filled the air all around; so quiet at first that one could barely hear it. As the tabby listened, the soft breath began to take on a regular in-and-out rhythm; more respiration than mechanical draft.

The breathing grew louder—one no longer had to strain to hear it. It swept over the collection of animals in a dreadful back-and-forth wind; the vital force of an angry Titan. Black dust swirled up to blast one way in union with the unseen monster's inhalation, only to quickly gust back in the opposing direction in keeping with the hot exhalation.

The General, using the heated wind to locate the point of origin from where the beast breathed, faced the southern sky. "Wall formation!" she called to her soldiers. "Bear—get the cat and go behind an elephant!"

The grizzly snatched up the tabby. Clutching Kitten to his chest, he ran behind the biggest bull elephant and stood upright. The other animals formed themselves into a single row; the pair of golden eagles perched atop the two elephants who stood in the center of the line.

The General positioned herself in the middle of the group of four wolves. "Wait," she said. "The thing will show itself soon."

The canid's intuition was right. Against the fading purple of the heavens, a monstrous shadow began to form; a murky fog too big to be a living creature. But it breathed—the huge darkness must have been living, at least in some way.

Rapidly expanding to fill the southern quadrant of the sky, the Stygian mist swirled with currents of deepest black; overwhelming the landscape with its shadowy mass. The violent wind-breathing stopped, and airborne ash began to settle over the line of animals, who could feel a peculiar vibration coming from deep within the earth. This shaking wasn't like an earthquake, or in any way reminiscent of the pounding of a rhino stampede; no—it seemed very much like the ground was trembling in fear; though of course, such a thing was not possible.

The eagles puffed out their feathers and began to shift their feet nervously up and down against the thick hides of their elephant friends. "This is not good," one of the birds announced. "I see ice out there, and it's moving; moving fast."

Wolf focused her sharp eyes on the southern horizon. "It's not just moving—it's growing."

The dark fog was touching down to earth about a mile from the animal troop. The ground had frozen at that point, and was covered by a thick layer of gleaming white ice. The leading edge of the frozen water was spreading forward and out at near-lightning speed, and before any of the creatures could even think about reacting, it had surrounded the General and her company with a solid boundary of subzero matter several feet high.

The elephants began to shiver violently. Kitten, fluffing out his striped coat in an effort to expand his thermal layer, looked at the trembling hindquarters of the big quadruped before him and feared for the creature's life; knowing that this type of animal was not built to withstand such severe cold. Even the thick-furred wolves and grizzlies were shaking under the assault of the bitter temperature; one lower than the deadly climate produced by a flesh-freezing Antarctica winter.

The female rhino began to grunt softly. Her feet had taken on an ugly look of death; as though the living matter had crystallized into black ice, turning the creature's warm blood to frosty slush. Wolf's eyelids drooped; her breathing had become much too slow.

Bear crumpled, falling onto the hard-frozen ground with Kitten clutched in his stiff arms. Animals were tumbling down all along the line, struck by the unconsciousness that precedes death by freezing, but somehow, the little cat was only very, very cold.

The tabby struggled to escape from the grizzly's rigid arms, and finally managed to free himself. Leaping high onto the top of the ice mass, the feline faced the giant shadow that blocked the southern sky. "Flöbbertigôbbet!" the tiny tiger shouted.

A faint blue fire flashed in the center of the dark cloud.

"I know what you want. I'll come with you—just let my friends live!"

The sapphire light sparkled. There was no answer.

"If you let them die, I won't join you!"

The blue fire shifted into red, and a deep sigh came from within the cloud. "I can't save them from death," a disembodied voice stated. "I can, however, keep the rest of the hemisphere from freezing. Come along with me, and I will spare the others."

"No deal. Resuscitate my friends now!"

"I cannot restore life, Kitten."

"You told me once that you could heal the sick."

"They're not sick—they're dead."

"Dead?" The feline collapsed onto the ice. "No, no, no!"

"Come with me, little cat. It's the only way to save the rest of the natural world."

The tabby lay facedown, rendered immobile by grief. Wolf dead, Bear dead, Pony dead, First Horse dead; the elephants, the rhinos, the lion, the other brave animals—all dead. The tiny tiger tried to press himself into the glacial mass beneath him, wishing he could freeze to death with his friends.

"Kitten," the cloud said, "if you continue to lie there, others will die. Get up, walk forward; join me, son."

The feline turned his head so that his left cheek was pressed against the ice as he stared dully into the blackness of night. Twilight had vanished; the heavens now studded with bright stars whose absence in the southern sky betrayed the presence of the evil fog. The cat's listless eyes detected a peculiar flashing in the distance, and he lifted himself onto his forelegs and looked up.

In the northern quadrant of the heavenly vault, one of the multitude of stars had begun to pulsate with a rich golden light. Kitten blinked in surprise. "Stars aren't usually gold like that," he said to himself. As he tried to focus his eyes more sharply on the distant celestial body, it exploded into a brilliant supernova that flooded the landscape with blinding illumination and intense heat.

Kitten instinctively went down into a low crouch to avoid having his vital organs burnt by the flash. The dazzling brilliance was gone almost immediately, and normal darkness returned. The cat tossed his head in astonishment. "Well—as hot as that was, it didn't feel bad, in fact; it felt good." He closed his eyes as another brief flash of golden light came, stronger than the first. The ice was instantly vaporized; leaving behind nothing but a sweet, warm fog.

As the layer of glacial footing vanished from beneath the tabby, he fell to the ground and rolled once. He felt the earth: it was no longer frozen. The feline looked into the southern sky, where stars were now visible—the Flöbbertigôbbet had gone.

Kitten rose to his feet, turning as he heard a soft rustle behind him. The phoenix stood there, lighting the area with the constant glow that emanated from his brilliant plumage. The tabby inhaled deeply, uplifted by the bird's subtle fragrance of cinnamon and frankincense. "Hello," the tiny tiger said.

"Hello, Kittenus Maximus," the phoenix replied.

"My friends are dead!" The cat was desperate. "You have more power than the Flöbbertigôbbet. Can you do anything?"

"Yes." The phoenix turned to look at the bodies behind him. "Dear brave soldiers," he whispered. One by one, the bird went to each corpse and exhaled a small purple flame onto its forehead. As he did so, the animals began to stir and breathe.

The female rhino rose up onto her feet; the three-toed appendages no longer blackened with frostbite. She walked to the phoenix and bowed before him in humble thanks; too awed to give voice to her gratitude. "You're welcome," the bird said.

The wolf managed to address the phoenix. "Sir—I was dead," she stated.

"Yes, ma'am," the bird replied.

"I don't think you should be calling me 'ma'am,' sir. I saw what you did while I was out of my body."

"We oppose the same enemy, Wolf, and I am not a military officer of higher rank than yours, so I believe the respectful address is appropriate."

"You are not the phoenix I know of from legend," Wolf said. "Who are you?"

"A visitor."

"That is rather vague, sir."

"I will be no more specific than that, ma'am."

"I see." The General looked down at the ground. The bird's illumination cast a soft light onto the burnt earth; the shimmering glow causing the shadows of rocks and pebbles to dance under the shifting light. Wolf looked at her feet, and marveled at how they had been thoroughly dead and cold as she floated above her body in the spiritual form used by the recently departed. Those calloused paws were useful again; warm and alive: able to carry her to yet more battles against the adversary. "You say we oppose the same enemy." The canid raised her head and gazed into the sparkling black eyes of the phoenix. "Does he threaten the place from which you are visiting?"

"No. He has no power there."

"There's a place where he has no power? How is that possible?"

"My time here is limited, General, and I need to use it to get the cat back to his home." The phoenix turned to the tabby. "Say your good-byes, Kittenus Maximus. Keep in mind that you will be returning to this place, and let no one grieve over your departure."

Kitten did as he was told; saying farewell to each of his dear friends and indulging in a great deal of feline-style cheek-rubbing as he did so. When he came to Wolf, he almost forgot the phoenix's command that no one should grieve. This creature was his mother now, and to leave her side caused him a pain akin to having a knife thrust into his heart. "I'll be back very soon, ma'am," the tiny tiger said, struggling to keep his composure.

"That fellow says you will return," the canid glanced at the glowing bird, "and I believe it. I'll miss you greatly, son, but I shall look forward to seeing you again."

"Let us go, Kittenus Maximus! I don't have much time!" The phoenix opened his wings and spread them wide. "Come sit at my feet."

After giving Wolf a parting lick of affection on her chin, the tabby ran to the bird and sat in the assigned spot. The One leaned down over the cat and brought his wings in; covering Kitten with his glowing form. The phoenix breathed out once, then inhaled deeply, and the pair was gone.

CHAPTER NINE

A Revelation

The phoenix straightened up and opened his wings. "We're here, Kittenus Maximus."

The tabby was amazed, seeing the emerald-leaved trees all around him. "How did you do that? All I did was blink once, and we're here!"

"The answer to that question would be impossible for you to understand. It's not that you lack intelligence, young fellow, but your brain, with its limited functions which are only suited to life in material worlds—it would not be able to grasp the basic concepts of a super-substantial dimension."

"I'm not sure I like that particular answer so very much," Kitten muttered.

"Please don't take it as an insult."

"I'll try not to," the tabby replied shortly. "So— we're back at the emerald grove. Where is the Door?"

"We'll have to go through the Void to get there."

"The awful nothing place?"

"Yes."

"Oh, dear. That was very nasty the first time. I don't expect the second trip will be much better."

"It will be easier with me at your side."

"Good." Kitten looked up at the bird, meeting the sparkling black eyes in a direct stare. "I know you're in a hurry, so I'll get right to the point."

"The point? What point would that be?"

"I've seen how much power you have. The Flöbbertigôbbet runs like a frightened mouse every time you show up. You bring the dead back to life and travel great distances in the blink of an eye. You can make stars explode into benign supernovas that cause glaciers to melt and evaporate into harmless fog. I have no doubt that you could easily free both my world and this one from the hold of the Flöbbertigôbbet if you chose to. Why haven't you done that?"

The phoenix lowered his gaze, avoiding the cat's eyes. "I'm sorry."

"You're sorry? That's all you can say: 'I'm sorry'? Savage acts of murder and destruction, twisted cruelty and horrible atrocities are carried out with feeble opposition from well-intentioned but helpless creatures who make a progress so tiny as to be nearly invisible when one gesture from you could end all the suffering. Why do you let it go on?"

The One looked up at the glittering leaves of the emerald trees.

"Don't stare into the bloody foliage—look me in the eye and give me a straight answer! What kind of perverse being would stand by with the power to help and do nothing? What is wrong with you?"

The phoenix looked the tabby straight in his furious eyes. "I am not doing nothing, Kittenus Maximus. I have transformed you so that you can fight the evil."

"Transformed me? I don't see any transformation. I'm still just a bloody tiny cat!"

"You are chewing out, as some might say, a being whom many would consider to be an awe-inspiring god. You have stood up to the Flöbbertigôbbet himself in the same bold way. Do you really believe that you are just a 'bloody tiny cat' and no more than the total value of that container of fur and flesh which holds you?"

"That answer is not acceptable! The fact remains that you have the power to instantly end the excessive suffering created by the Flöbbertigôbbet but you have chosen to shift the burden onto creatures with no power."

"You have power, Kittenus Maximus—you can change things! And don't ask me why I haven't solved the problems—instead, ask the people of your world why so many members of their species play along with evil."

"The people in my world can't hear animals when they ask questions. If they could, horses wouldn't end up on dinner plates." The tabby snarled in frustration. "This conversation is pointless—kindly get me out of here."

"You will see," The One said. "You will see."

"Yeah, right!" the little tiger snapped.

"Sit still and be quiet!" the phoenix ordered.

Growling in a low tone, the angry Kitten tried to contain himself. The bird stood over him, head lowered, and closed his eyes. As the tabby watched, the grove began to dissipate into fragments of shattered green shot through with fuzzy black. There was a nasty screeching sound, the solid traces of the forest vanished, and Kitten and the phoenix entered the Void.

The tabby shuddered when the ground disappeared out from under him. He didn't fall, there being no gravity in the awful Nowhere, but the feeling of suspension in an icy vacuum bereft of matter and spatial relationships was certainly nothing to be enjoyed. The little cat winced, trying to be grateful for the fact that this time he seemed to have a body, and was able to remember who he was.

He spotted something in front of him: slight hints of grey were showing against the black of the vacuum. A moment later, the wall and its carved stone face appeared, and something resembling physical order was restored. Kitten felt a warm body beneath him: the phoenix was supporting the tabby on one gold-feathered shoulder. "Go through the Door, Kittenus Maximus," The One commanded.

"I'm sorry I yelled at you," the cat said. His temper had cooled off quickly, and he was genuinely contrite.

"I understand," the bird replied. "Now go through the Door, please. The mouth will open to accommodate you."

The feline put his head to the stone lips of the face and poked his nose into the expanding opening. He could see his Lady's library, and executed a great kick forward; pushing off against the phoenix's shoulder. Falling through over the books, the cat tumbled onto the carpet. He looked back to say good-bye to The One, but the Door had vanished into the smooth boards of the wall.

The little tiger lay on the carpet and took a long, deep breath; overwhelmed by sudden joy. It was so good to once again smell the familiar fragrance of home: the friendly mustiness of the old great house as expressed here in the grand library. Its unique bouquet was made up of many fine ingredients: the sweet earthy scent of fog-fed molds which grew in dark, unreachable corners; the slightly scratchy old-wool redolence of eighteenth-century rugs that had comforted the feet of the countless visitors who came to the book-lined room; the soft aroma of precious antique volumes whose exquisite bindings held handmade vellum pages. The singular perfume of the athenæum was very pleasing to the cat's nose.

Kitten looked at his favorite window. It was sunset —the birds would be having their late supper of freshly served-up seeds now.

The tabby ran to his stool. As his face appeared at the window glass, a tremendous cheer went up from outside. Birds too numerous to count were covering the branches of the huge yew tree and its oak neighbors, and on the ground below, scores of forest creatures were crowded together on Lady's manicured grass. All were looking at Kitten as they yelped, sang, squeaked, and chattered in exultant celebration.

Dove flew down from the yew and landed on the window sill. "Sir feline! You have returned! We've been waiting for you." She flapped her wings against her body and let out a brief but heart-thrilling song of joy. "This is wonderful!"

"Yes, it is!" Kitten replied.

"If you had been gone one more day, I would have come after you! And these animals here: they were all so impressed by the courage you displayed by going through the Door that they were going to come along with me."

"I came back to make certain you would not do that, Dove. The other world is an amazing place, but it's very dangerous."

"You look different somehow, sir feline."

"Please—call me Kitten."

"You seem changed, Kitten."

"How so?"

"It's hard to say—you just don't look quite the same." Dove's eyes sparkled with excitement. "Did you find the Flöbbertigôbbet? What was the other world like?"

"Now, there's a story!" Kitten looked out at the animals pressed together on his Lady's lawn. The window before him was open a crack to let in fresh air; its latch undone. "Let's get this window opened wider so all can hear me. Is there anyone out there clever and strong enough to raise this sash?"

Kitten scanned the crowd—not a brown bear in sight; their breed having become extinct in England sometime before the eleventh century. A couple of big English beavers with dexterous paws would have been handy fellows to have nearby, but they too had been wiped out long ago, with the exception of one lone wild beaver recently spotted felling a tree by a distant river.

The tabby scanned the group of animals, becoming increasingly frustrated by his search for help. "Not even one single wild boar left on this little island of ours," the tiny tiger muttered. "A strong-necked animal like that could lift this sash in a quick second." As the cat's gaze roamed over the wildlife assortment, his heart crumpled in response to the total absence of wolves; a species not seen running free in this nation since Tudor times. "What has become of my sweet country home?" the tabby sighed. "The magical howl of the wolf, that song which has the power to thaw hard-frozen spirits of solid ice if listened to with an open, quiet ear; not heard on my fair isle for centuries." Kitten continued to scan the representative crowd of what was left of England's natural beasts; his eyes lighting up when he spotted a group of otters. "You there!" he shouted through the glass.

"Eh?" One of the sleek, slender fellows stood upright on his hind legs and cocked his head to the side, regarding the little cat with bright-eyed intelligence. "Are you addressing me, sir?"

"Yes! Can you and your friends come raise this window sash, please?"

"Straightaway, sir!" The otter dropped to all fours and bounded gracefully to the window, followed by a group of six brethren. Dove left the sill to give them room to work, and the seven joined together with their clever webbed feet and had the window sash raised in very little time.

"Thank you so much, gentlemen," Kitten said.

"Our pleasure, sir!" seven otter voices chimed in unison.

"Now," the tabby announced, "if you would all please move in closer, I shall tell you the story of the other world."

"And then I fell back into the library," Kitten bowed his head, "and that was that."

"Extraordinary!" Dove declared. "Absolutely extraordinary!"

The crowd of wild creatures was silent as all sat in the quiet darkness of the forest night and considered the tale which had been told to them. Kitten looked out at his audience. "What do you think?"

"As I said before, it's extraordinary," Dove replied.

"I'm amazed," a badger mumbled.

"It's incredible!" a hare cried.

"The phoenix told you that you're destined to fight the Flöbbertigôbbet in our world and the other one," Dove said to the little cat. "How are you going to go about fighting him here?"

The tabby considered this question for a moment. "I have to learn more about the ways in which his power is manifested in this world."

"Well," Dove said, "I suggest that you study people, then."

"People?"

"Yes. I'm not saying, mind you, that all people are evil, Kitten, because they aren't; but the story you just told us about the other world—in that place, the Flöbbertigôbbet preys upon animals not because he needs to, but because he wants to. That same evil happens here, with the actions carried out by humans."

"Yes." Kitten nodded in agreement. "I've heard about that."

"One particularly cold-blooded example comes to mind at this moment," Dove said. "I learned about this watching your Lady's news broadcast through her window. Did you know there's a global moratorium on whaling?"

"No."

"Well, there is, and Japan is ignoring it. They launched a hunt in the Pacific, where they killed endangered whales for the sole purpose of selling the meat on the Japanese 'luxury food' market. Their ships recently went back to port with almost a hundred dead bodies."

The feline was stunned by this news. "They slaughtered endangered animals just so rich people could eat them?"

"Yes—and they're going to do it again. They've been doing it regularly for many years."

Kitten closed his eyes, imagining the hunt: churning sea waters; fast boats filled with greedy men. Barbed harpoons would be shot into the great mammals of the deep, who would spin frantically and dive; trying to escape the murderers who pursued them relentlessly. Deep in his mind, the tabby could hear the final songs of the bleeding whales; the haunting cries of the creatures who would die so that jaded human palates might enjoy an exotic high-status treat. The little cat trembled with ill-controlled rage. "So! So—even now, in this modern century, in a country which is thought to be civilized—this is what people are capable of. I suppose I must find some way to fight that human capability."

"How will you do that? I'm sorry, Kitten, but you're just an animal; just a cat. I don't wish to be unduly negative, but I think; perhaps the phoenix who gave you the assignment to fight evil in this world—maybe he doesn't understand the position of animals here. With the incredible power he's accustomed to wielding, he may be out of touch with our reality; our role in a world where humans set themselves up as supreme beings and we are, well—when all is said and done, we're just products, stock: items to be sold, bought, and consumed. Endangered wild creatures or domestic livestock: we are in the end entirely helpless; without any voice whatsoever in this world. It's possible that the phoenix doesn't fully understand our position."

"You could be right, ma'am. I admit that when I apologized to The One for having insulted him, my apology was sincere to the point that I believe he truly means well. I don't, however, believe he's infallible. Who is?" The little tiger wore a thoroughly dejected look on his face; so obviously let down that it almost seemed as though his crisp white whiskers had turned limp. "You're right, ma'am—I'm just a cat; with no more influence in this world than those poor dead whales."

Dove's head suddenly shot straight up. "Scatter!" she cried, and in a flash, she and the other woodland creatures fled; vanishing into the cover of the forest.

"What?" Kitten listened carefully, and could hear thumping footsteps coming down the corridor toward the library.

The book-room's door opened, and the Lady entered. She wore her usual riding clothes: sack-like brown sweater, close-fitting beige breeches, tall black boots whose inner shafts were lathered with foamy horse sweat. The middle-aged woman's dark, almost black hair was pulled back into a low ponytail at the nape of her neck, and the skin of her otherwise smooth high forehead bore a horizontal imprint from the close pressure of a snug riding helmet. Despite the rather haggish outfit and dent across her brow, Lady was beautiful; with big long-lashed eyes of gentle green, and a fresh ivory complexion only lightly touched by time.

She carried a burning candle set in a small antique-silver holder. Kitten was well acquainted with his Lady's moods, and knew that when she carried a lit taper instead of switching on the household lighting, she was feeling poorly and having one of those days when electricity offended her to an extreme degree. Lady was by no means a conformist, and generally thought modern technology to be more curse than blessing. When she was truly depressed, she saw wired devices as the work of lazy devils, and would have none of such things.

The woman strode across the room toward the mahogany cabinet which held the fine liquors she offered to house guests. "I hope Harry didn't drink the last of my best Scotch," she muttered. "I need it. Kitten's never coming back; never!" She set her candle atop the cabinet and, locating the crystal dispenser she sought, poured herself a half-glass of the potent brown liquid. After tossing down a generous mouthful, she turned; feeling a draught of cold night air. "How did that window get wide open?" Setting her drink on a nearby table, she picked up the candle and walked forward.

Kitten sat on his stool and watched as his Lady approached. The candlelight was dim, and the weary

229

equestrienne didn't notice the little feline until she was nearly upon him. Seeing the reflection of the flame-glow glittering in the tabby's amber eyes, she became aware of his presence. "Kitten! You're back! I don't believe it—you've come back!"

Lady set the candlestick on the floor and scooped her beloved pet into her arms. "Oh, my sweet angel—I haven't been able to sleep without you at my side! Where have you been for so long?"

"Well, milady," Kitten replied, "I went to another world."

The woman's finely muscled arms became rigid, and her breath froze in her throat as she stopped breathing. Her grip on the tabby grew tighter, and Kitten began to fear the athletic female would crush him. "Lady!" he cried. "Let me go!"

Letting go was not a problem. The aristocrat's eyes rolled back in her head as she let out her tightly held breath and began to fall to the floor; thoroughly unconscious from the shock of hearing clearly enunciated speech come forth from the tiny mouth of a Shorthair Classic Tabby. Her arms fell open like the helpless limbs of a rag doll, and the little cat was freed into midair as his owner's body plummeted towards the floor, hitting the carpeted surface with a muted thud.

Landing on his feet, Kitten looked at the lump of insensible humanity that lay face-up on the rug. "Well!" the tiny tiger whispered. "I've got some measure of influence now, haven't I?" Stepping up next to the woman's head, the feline began to gently lick her cheek; trying to revive her. "Yes!" the cat declared between tongue strokes. "I have a voice!"

THE END—FOR NOW

Thank you for reading "Where Wolves Talk."
As an independent author, I rely upon readers to spread the word about
my work. If you enjoyed this story, please consider leaving a brief
review on this book's page at Amazon.

Made in the USA
Lexington, KY
15 September 2015